She was there. The woman who had haunted Zac's sleep for so long.

Zac had a sense of having been injured, and her voice was like a siren's song with the power to lead him from the darkness. Or lure him more deeply into it.

"Who did this to you? Who would want to kill you? I know how much is at stake, yet when I thought you were dead..." she whispered.

For a split second Zac could have sworn he felt her lips against his.

"Why did you come? Why did it have to be *you?*" She spoke once more.

She paused again, and Zac could hear the pounding of her heart. Or was that his own?

"I can't let any of that matter," she said harshly. "You can't die on me, Zac. I have a job to do. I have to find out why you're here, so I need you alive...."

Dear Harlequin Intrigue Reader,

As you make travel plans for the summer, don't forget to pack along this month's exciting new Harlequin Intrigue books!

The notion of being able to rewrite history has always been fascinating, so be sure to check out *Secret Passage* by Amanda Stevens. In this wildly innovative third installment in QUANTUM MEN, supersoldier Zac Riley must complete a vital mission, but his long-lost love is on a crucial mission of her own! Opposites combust in *Wanted Woman* by B.J. Daniels, which pits a beautiful daredevil on the run against a fiercely protective deputy sheriff—the next book in CASCADES CONCEALED.

Julie Miller revisits THE TAYLOR CLAN when one of Kansas City's finest infiltrates a crime boss's compound and finds himself under the dangerous spell of an aristocratic beauty. Will he be the *Last Man Standing?* And in *Legally Binding* by Ann Voss Peterson—the second sizzling story in our female-driven in-line continuity SHOTGUN SALLYS—a reformed bad boy rancher needs the help of the best female legal eagle in Texas to clear him of murder!

Who can resist those COWBOY COPS? In our latest offering in our Western-themed promotion, Adrianne Lee tantalizes with *Denim Detective*. This gripping family-in-jeopardy tale has a small-town sheriff riding to the rescue, but he's about to learn one doozy of a secret.... And finally this month you are cordially invited to partake in *Her Royal Bodyguard* by Joyce Sullivan, an enchanting mystery about a commoner who discovers she's a betrothed princess and teams up with an enigmatic bodyguard who vows to protect her from evildoers.

Enjoy our fabulous lineup this month!

Sincerely,

Denise O'Sullivan
Senior Editor, Harlequin Intrigue

SECRET PASSAGE
AMANDA STEVENS

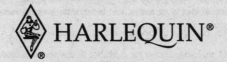

HARLEQUIN®

TORONTO • NEW YORK • LONDON
AMSTERDAM • PARIS • SYDNEY • HAMBURG
STOCKHOLM • ATHENS • TOKYO • MILAN • MADRID
PRAGUE • WARSAW • BUDAPEST • AUCKLAND

ISBN 0-373-22777-9

SECRET PASSAGE

ABOUT THE AUTHOR

Amanda Stevens is the bestselling author of over thirty novels of romantic suspense. In addition to being a Romance Writers of America RITA® Award finalist, she is also the recipient of awards in Career Achievement in Romantic/Mystery and Career Achievement in Romantic/Suspense from *Romantic Times* magazine. She currently resides in Texas. To find out more about past, present and future projects, please visit her Web site at www.amandastevens.com.

Books by Amanda Stevens

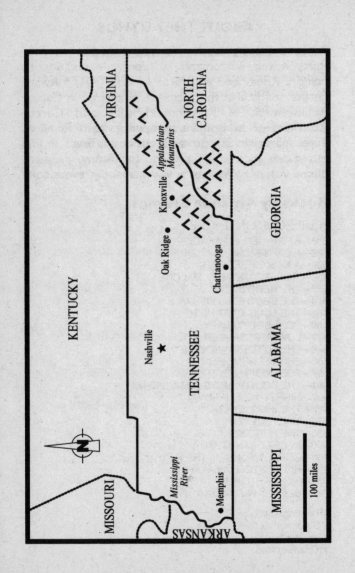

CAST OF CHARACTERS

Camille Somersby—She will do anything to protect her grandfather—and the future—even if it means deceiving the only man she's ever loved.

Zac Riley—A supersoldier who will go to extraordinary lengths to carry out his mission.

Dr. Von Meter—A megalomaniac who has destroyed lives for over sixty years.

Dr. Kessler—The only one standing in Von Meter's way.

Roth Vogel—A supersoldier with his own agenda.

Alice Nichols—A woman who knows how to get what she wants.

Special Agent Talbott—Is the FBI agent a pawn in a deadly game or a man who is willing to betray his own country?

Betty Wilson—A nurse who has more than a professional interest in Zac.

Daniel Clutter—A widower who becomes all too susceptible to Alice Nichols's charms.

Adam—Can the memory of his five-year-old son save Zac?

Prologue

The Secret City,
1943

Her cover was blown. She had no proof, of course, only a nagging suspicion that she was being watched.

Sliding her hand inside her purse, Camille Somersby let the cool, deadly feel of the Colt .45 bolster her courage as she hurried out to her car. Climbing inside, she slammed the door, started the engine and then struggled with the gears for a moment before easing the Studebaker from the muddy parking area onto the street.

As she made the first corner, she glanced in the rearview mirror. She didn't think she'd picked up a tail, but she couldn't be sure. In wartime, spies were everywhere. Especially here, in a place the locals called the Secret City.

Nestled in a picturesque East Tennessee valley surrounded by tree-lined ridges, the city—which did not exist on any map—was isolated from the outside world, despite its proximity to Knoxville.

Complete with stores, schools, a church, hospital, newspaper and both single and multifamily dwellings, the whole community had been built practically overnight by the Army Corps of Engineers to accommodate the thousands of scientists, engineers and plant personnel employed at three top secret facilities known only by their code names—X-10, Y-12 and K-25.

Security around the perimeter of the city was tight. The borders were patrolled around the clock, and no one was allowed to enter or leave without a pass. Phone calls were monitored and mail routinely censored. In such an environment, fear and suspicion were bound to run rampant.

And maybe that was all it was, Camille decided. This feeling of being watched. It could well be nothing more than her own paranoia at work. The burden of her own secrets wearing on her nerves.

Ostensibly, she was one of hundreds of young women who'd poured into the area seeking employment on the government reservation. But, in reality, Camille had been sent to observe a smaller and even more highly classified entity known as

Project Rainbow. The unit was run by Dr. Nicholas Kessler, a world-renowned scientist whose research into electromagnetic fields had attracted the military's attention at the start of the war.

He didn't know it yet, but Dr. Kessler's future was irrevocably tied to Camille's. She had been sent to protect him, but if her cover had been compromised, the whole mission could be in jeopardy. It would be difficult to insure Dr. Kessler's safety if she ended up dead in an alley somewhere.

Grimacing at the image, she shot another glance over her shoulder as she approached the gate. Flashing her pass at the guard, she waited for him to lift the barricade, then smiled and waved as she drove through.

Outside the barbed-wire fence, she relaxed a bit as she headed north toward Ashton, a small community five miles away where she'd been fortunate enough to find a cottage for rent. The massive influx of workers to the area had quickly eaten up all the government housing so that newcomers were forced to seek accommodations outside the reservation. Those commuting back and forth not only had to contend with the resentment of the locals, but with gas rationing and long lines of traffic to and from the project.

Camille had been worried at first that living away

from the city might hamper her ability to carry out her mission, but so far it had worked out rather well. Ashton was a small, close-knit community, and she knew that if anyone suspicious showed up in the vicinity asking the wrong questions, she was bound to hear about it.

She'd also quickly come to appreciate the tranquility of the cottage. The house was situated on a lake, and the breezes blowing in from the water at night reminded her of happier times. When Adam was still alive.

Even after all this time, the thought of her son still brought quick tears. He'd been gone for over a year, but the pain was still as sharp and deep as the day she'd lost him. The only thing that had changed was her anger. It seemed to grow stronger and more consuming with each passing day. Anger at herself for not being able to protect him. Anger at the person who was ultimately responsible for his death.

And anger at the one man who might have been able to prevent it.

An image of that man slipped through the walls Camille had built around her heart, and, for a moment, she remembered too much. Dark eyes and a deep voice. Strong hands and a knowing touch.

The way he'd held her in the darkness. The way

he'd kissed her, caressed her, moved her in ways no man had ever moved her before.

He'd been the love of her life.

And now he no longer remembered her.

But there had to be something left of his feelings for her, Camille thought bitterly. Some buried remnant of emotion that she could use to her advantage when he showed up here.

And he would come. She knew it without a doubt. That was the reason she'd been sent here, after all. To find out what he was up to and then, if necessary, stop him at any cost.

At any cost.

Her hands gripped the wheel as she thought about what that might entail. Lies. Deception. *Murder.*

Camille began to tremble. Taking a life, even in wartime, wasn't something she contemplated lightly. Taking the life of a man she'd once loved so deeply would surely earn her a very special place in hell.

So be it. He was the enemy now.

God help her—God help them all—if she forgot that fact even for a second.

Chapter One

It was the fourth night in a row the old man had come into Blue Monday's. Zac Riley supposed he should be grateful the club had attracted a new customer. God knows there'd been few enough of those, young or old, in recent months, and if traffic didn't pick up, he'd soon be out of a job. Again.

Still, a guy who looked to have one foot in the grave was hardly the target clientele of a waterfront blues club. And there was something about the man, apart from his age, that gave Zac the creeps. He didn't know why, exactly, but he figured it had something to do with the dream. The sudden reoccurrence of the nightmare coincided with the old man's first appearance in the club. And Zac had had the dream every night since.

The details never varied. He was always trapped in a cold, dark, windowless place with no way out. He could hear the clanking of metal, the steady drip of water and, in the distance, screams.

But upon awakening, what Zac always recalled most vividly about the dream was his fear. A mind-numbing terror like nothing he'd ever known before.

Afterward he would lie awake for hours, not daring to fall back asleep. But sometimes he'd drift off in spite of himself and that's when she would come. A woman shrouded by mist. A temptress who beckoned and enticed but always remained maddeningly elusive, just out of Zac's reach.

He had no idea if she was real or not. Maybe she was someone he'd known a long time ago—a lifetime ago—before the accident had wiped out a good portion of his memory. Or maybe she was nothing but a fantasy, a dream lover conjured out of fear and desperation.

Whoever she was, *whatever* she was, she'd haunted Zac's sleep for years.

And now he had the sudden, unaccountable notion that she and the old man were somehow connected.

A chill rode up his spine as he tracked the man's labored progress to the end of the bar where he perched, with no small effort, on a stool, then sat with arms folded, head bowed, waiting.

What's your story? Zac wondered.

What was a guy like that doing in a place like this? The drinks were watery, the atmosphere gloomy, the location on the dark and sleazy fringes of hip and pricey South Street. There were hundreds of bars scattered all over the City of Brotherly Love. What had brought him to this one?

Zac didn't think the old guy was homeless. He tipped too generously to be down on his luck, but he had the look of a man that time had forgotten. His heavy wool overcoat was threadbare in places, but Zac suspected it had once been quite elegant, perhaps custom-made for the man's tall, slender physique.

Zac waited a couple of beats, then ambled to the end of the bar. Wiping off the mahogany surface, he said cheerfully, ''What'll it be tonight?''

''Whiskey,'' the man muttered without looking up.

His raspy voice was like nails on a chalkboard to Zac. He poured the whiskey, then slid the drink across the bar. As the old man's skeletal fingers closed around the glass, he glanced up. His eyes were the color of night. Dark, cold, scary.

Disconcerted by the man's stare, Zac started to

turn away, then paused. "Do I know you? Have we met before?"

The old man lifted his whiskey. "Do you think we've met before?"

Zac tried to laugh off his uneasiness. "Now you sound like a shrink."

The old man lowered his empty glass. "I'm not a shrink. I'm a scientist."

"A scientist, huh? We don't get many of those in here." Zac scrubbed at an invisible ring on the bar. "So what brings an educated man like yourself to a dump like this?"

"You do, Zac."

The hair at the back of Zac's neck rose. "How do you know my name?"

The dark eyes gleamed in the murky light. "I know a lot about you. Probably more than you know about yourself."

"Is that right?" Zac felt the first stirrings of anger. And maybe even a touch of fear. "How do you figure that?"

"Because I'm the man who created you."

Something tightened around Zac's heart. Like a fist trying to squeeze the life out of him. "What the hell is that supposed to mean?" he demanded, thoroughly unnerved now by the stranger.

The man smiled slightly as he fished a card from

his coat pocket and laid it on the bar. Zac glanced down in spite of himself. Dr. Joseph Von Meter. The address was in the Chestnut Hill area, a historic neighborhood about as far removed from Blue Monday's as one could imagine.

Zac lifted his gaze. "You're a long way from home, old man."

"As are you, Zac. You have no idea."

HE CAME BACK THE NEXT NIGHT. And the next two nights after that. It was easy to avoid him on the weekend. The live music of Blue Monday's attracted a noisy crowd—aging hippies for the most part and some suburbanites in town for a night of drinking and slumming. Zac kept his distance, allowing the new bartender to wait on the strange old man.

But the place was empty again on Sunday night, and Zac was alone behind the bar when Von Meter showed up, precisely at nine, just like the other nights.

Bored and anxious to close up, Zac had been staring out the window when the limo pulled to the curb in front of the club. A uniformed driver got out and came around to open the back door, then reached a gloved hand down to help his passenger disembark.

Definitely not homeless, Zac thought, watching the old man shuffle through the snow.

The driver waited until his charge was at the door, then he got back in the car and drove off.

A blast of cold air followed Von Meter into the club. He wore the same rumpled suit under the same shabby overcoat with the same hat pulled low over his eyes. He hobbled to the end of the bar and took his usual seat even though the stools closer to the door were unoccupied. Folding his arms on the bar, he bowed his head and waited.

Zac's nerve endings tingled in apprehension as he studied the old man's profile, what he could see of it, and he berated himself for not closing up earlier. He hadn't had a customer all night. The snowstorm had kept everyone home, which was where he should have been hours ago. Had he subconsciously been waiting for Von Meter to show up?

"I know a lot about you. Probably more than you know about yourself."

"I'm the man who created you."

Telling himself he should throw the old goat out and be done with it, Zac walked slowly down the bar until he stood in front of Von Meter. "What'll it be tonight?"

"Whiskey," the old man rasped.

Zac poured the drink, then slid it across the bar.

As the man's wasted fingers closed around the glass, a feeling of déjà vu crept over Zac. They'd played this scene too many times before.

"How long do you plan on keeping this up?" he asked abruptly.

The old man set the empty glass on the table and lifted his gaze to Zac's. His eyes were darker than Zac remembered. Dark and cold and...somehow timeless. "Until you ask the right question."

Zac lifted an eyebrow. "Then why don't you save us both a lot of trouble and tell me what the right question is?"

The old man licked his lips, as if savoring the taste of the whiskey. "You don't remember much about your past, do you?"

"I don't remember you," Zac said. "But I get the impression you think we know each other. How did you put it? Oh, yeah. You're the man who created me. Next thing I know, you'll be telling me you're my long-lost father or something."

The dark eyes held Zac's gaze. "I'm not your father. But we are connected."

"How?"

He didn't answer immediately, but instead slid his glass across the counter for a refill. When Zac complied, the old man's gaze turned enigmatic. "Shall I tell you about the woman?"

Zac's blood froze and, for a moment, he couldn't speak. Couldn't even breathe. Then he said angrily, "What woman? What the hell are you talking about?"

"The woman you dream about. She's lovely, isn't she? Ethereal. Ghostlike. Too beautiful to be real."

Enough, Zac thought. Von Meter wasn't just creeping him out now. He was starting to scare him. And, apart from the nightmares, Zac didn't scare easily. "How do you know about her?"

The old man leaned across the bar. "I created her. I put her in your head. She was my gift to you."

"You created her, you created me. Who are you, God?"

Von Meter merely smiled at Zac's sarcasm and fished another card from his pocket. He laid it on the bar, faceup, and rose shakily to his feet. "Memories are a funny thing, Zac. In the right hands, they can be manipulated, suppressed, planted. How can you know what's real? And do you really want to know?"

"Look," Zac said angrily. "I don't know what kind of head games you're trying to play here, but I want no part of it. You come in here again, I'll throw you out. You understand?"

"I understand everything. And soon you will, too." With that, the old man shambled across the room to the front door and drew it open. Through the eddying snow, Zac caught a glimpse of the limo gliding to the curb, as if the driver had been summoned by a telepathic command. A moment later, they were gone.

FOR THE REST OF THE EVENING, Zac tried to ignore the warning bells clanging inside his head, the gnawing sensation in his gut that told him disaster lurked around the corner. As he got ready to close up, he tried to convince himself that Von Meter was just some weird old guy getting off by messing with his head.

But as the night wore on, so did Zac's uneasiness.

Locking up, he grabbed his coat, then paused on his way out as his gaze lit on the card still lying faceup on the bar. His first instinct was to toss it the way he had the other one, but, changing his mind, he grabbed it and stuffed it into his coat pocket as he headed out the door.

The snow was coming down harder now. Shivering in his lightweight jacket, Zac paused in front of the tattoo parlor next door to watch. Even in the garish lights, the flakes were beautiful. White. Crystalline. Dreamlike. Their delicate beauty reminded him of something…someone…

"I created her. I put her in your head. She was my gift to you."

Zac tried to conjure an image of the woman now, but suddenly she was more elusive than ever.

"Memories are a funny thing, Zac. In the right hands, they can be manipulated, suppressed, planted. How can you know what's real? And do you really want to know?"

Ducking his head from the cold, Zac hurried down the street. The wind blowing off the Delaware River was brutal tonight, but luckily, he didn't have far to go. The two-room flat he rented was just at the end of the street.

He was halfway home, lost in thought, when a cab pulled to the curb beside him. As Zac strode past, he could see that the driver was alone in the car. He sat slumped in the seat, arms folded, as if waiting for a fare.

But the streets were deserted.

Except for Zac.

His hands were in his pockets and he fingered the business card he'd stuffed in there earlier. He pulled it out now and gazed at the name and address under the streetlight.

Backtracking down the sidewalk, he rapped his

knuckles on the driver's window. "Hey, you waiting for somebody?"

The driver rolled down the glass. "Just you, buddy. Where you want to go?"

"Chestnut Hill." Zac gave the man the address, then asked about the fare. Whistling softly at the amount, he mentally counted the cash he had in his wallet. The trip would take about half of what he had on him—his life savings—but what the hell? Who needed to eat?

Climbing into the back of the cab, Zac leaned his head against the shabby upholstery, enjoying the warmth from the heater. He must have dozed off because it seemed like only moments later that the driver was rousing him.

"Hey, buddy, you awake back there?"

Zac sat up and rubbed his eyes. "Yeah, I'm awake." But he had the disconcerting notion that he had somehow been transported to a strange, new world. The neighborhood was one of those dreamy, Christmas-card-looking places made even more surreal by the swirling snow.

"Pretty swanky address, if you don't mind my saying so," the driver observed.

Yeah, Zac thought. *And why do I have the feeling I'm about to fall down a rabbit hole?*

He paid the man, then got out and stood for a

moment, gazing around. Von Meter's place was a three-story redbrick town house segregated from the street by an ornate wrought-iron fence. The gate had been left ajar, as if in anticipation of Zac's arrival.

He stepped into the courtyard, a frozen wonderland with icicles dripping from a fountain and stone statuary cloaked in snow. If possible the wind was harsher here than on the waterfront, and Zac hurried up the cobblestone walkway to ring the front bell. A uniformed maid promptly answered the door. "Yes?"

"My name is Zac Riley. I'm here to see Dr. Von Meter."

He wouldn't have been surprised if the young woman had turned him away, but instead she smiled and curtsied and beckoned him inside the warm house. "Please come in, Mr. Riley. Dr. Von Meter is expecting you."

"He is?"

"Why, yes, of course. May I take your coat?"

"No, I think I'll keep it if you don't mind." Never knew when you might need to make a speedy exit, Zac decided, his gaze taking in the luxurious surroundings.

The foyer was large and spacious with an inlaid wood floor, a magnificent, curving staircase and a domed skylight from which one could watch the clouds by day and the stars by night. Tonight, however, the etched glass was banked with snow, giving Zac a touch of claustrophobia.

The maid led him down a dim hallway to a set of ornate wooden doors, which she drew open after a discreet knock. The room inside was richly furnished in leather and tapestries and floor-to-ceiling bookcases packed with gilded tomes. It smelled of cigar smoke and old secrets.

Von Meter stood at the window, staring out.

"Mr. Riley is here to see you," the maid announced softly.

The old man didn't say a word, but a brief nod of his head seemed communication enough for the maid. She motioned Zac inside, then backed out of the room. Only when he heard the doors close did Von Meter finally turn.

He looked different tonight. His hair was a dingy white, like day-old snow, and his face was even leaner than Zac remembered, the frail, taut skin appearing to have the suppleness of parchment.

"This is some place," Zac said.

Von Meter smiled faintly. "It's old and drafty, but it suits my needs."

Something about the comment made Zac wonder if they'd had a similar conversation before. "It beats the dump I'm staying in now,'' he said with a shrug.

''Perhaps.'' The old man walked over to his desk and sat down, then gestured to a chair across from him. ''But your apartment has its attractions, does it not? I'm referring to the young lady in 3C, of course.''

The muscles in Zac's stomach tightened. ''How do you know about her?''

''The two of you have become quite close in recent weeks. I'm afraid that has to end. You can't afford the distraction.''

Zac leaped to his feet, the old man's presumption making him suddenly furious. ''What is this? How do you know about my personal life? How the hell do you know anything about me?''

Von Meter remained outwardly complacent. ''Please try to calm yourself. Everything will be clear to you soon.''

He pressed a button on his desk, and, a moment later, the maid opened the door. ''Yes?''

''Is Roth still here?''

''I believe he's in the solarium, sir.''

''Would you ask him to come in?''

''Of course.''

A moment later, the door opened again, and a tall, well-dressed man with a lean, muscular build strode through. His hair, a strange silvery color, was a striking counterpoint to the black turtleneck he wore, but the most remarkable thing about his appearance was the color of his eyes—one blue, one green and both cold as ice.

As their gazes collided, a shiver went up Zac's spine. He wasn't one for making snap judgments, but he had an immediate aversion to the man. In spite of the expensive clothes and carefully styled hair, there was something…unseemly about his appearance. As if the man's sinister nature lurked just beneath the surface, waiting to suck in the unsuspecting.

A nasty customer, Zac thought, and he'd met more than a few in his time.

As if reading his mind, the man smiled. "Well, well, well," he said in a voice that might have belonged to the devil himself. It was smooth, oily, decadent. "The infamous Zac Riley."

"You know me?" Zac said with a frown. If their paths had crossed, he was glad that memory hadn't survived.

"Perhaps the explanations are best left to Dr. Von Meter," the man suggested.

"Yes, perhaps they are," Von Meter agreed. He turned back to Zac. "This is Roth Vogel, Zac. He's here to assist in your briefing, but first, we need to get you settled. We have a room prepared for you upstairs. I'll send someone to your apartment to pack up your things—"

"Like hell you will." Zac shot to his feet. "I don't know what kind of scam you're trying to pull, old man, but I don't want any part of it."

He spun, but before he could cross the room, the door slammed shut, apparently of its own volition. He whipped around to find a gun pointed at his chest. His gaze lifted to Vogel's and the man's eyes gleamed in anticipation. Zac knew that look. He'd seen it before, on a man who'd tried to slit his throat in a dark alley one night for the twenty bucks he had in his wallet. *Tried* was the operative word.

"What the hell is this?" he asked through clenched teeth. "Some kind of shakedown? I hate to disappoint you, but I've got about ten bucks in my pocket. You think you can take it, have at it," he challenged Vogel.

"Put that thing away," Von Meter barked. "There is no need for violence." When Vogel reluctantly complied, the old man said to Zac, "I apologize. You aren't a prisoner here. You're free to leave any time you wish."

"In that case, *hasta la vista*." He gave them both a quick salute.

A muscle twitched at the corner of Vogel's left

eye—the blue one—as if he was having a very hard time suppressing his temper. Or his trigger finger.

A nasty customer indeed, Zac thought as he strode through the doorway and down the hallway to the foyer, expecting to hear, at any moment, the sound of footsteps in hot pursuit. But no one followed him or tried to stop him as he drew open the front door and walked out.

Once on the frosty street, he hailed a taxi, climbed into the back seat, then, before they could drive off, he got out again. Ignoring the driver's indignant curse, Zac returned to the house and rang the bell. The same maid answered the door, and this time Zac let her take his coat. When she showed him to the study, Von Meter was alone once more.

"Allow me to apologize again for Roth's behavior." He motioned Zac to a seat.

"What the hell was that all about?" Zac demanded.

Distaste flickered across Von Meter's face. "You're referring to the gun."

"And the slamming door. How'd you manage that little trick?"

"It wasn't a trick. Roth is a very gifted telekinetic."

"A telekinetic, huh? And here I thought he was just your everyday asshole."

"He is temperamental, I'll grant you that. Impulsive. Insubordinate. Ambitious. A loose cannon, I believe is the term used these days." Von Meter sighed. "But he has his uses."

"Forget about Vogel," Zac said bluntly. "What do you want from me?"

"I want to help you," Von Meter replied. "You want to know about your past. I can supply the missing details. But first, I need to know what you do remember."

"Why?"

"How would I know where to begin, otherwise?"

Zac supposed the explanation was logical enough, but he still didn't trust the old man. "I don't remember much," he admitted reluctantly. "My parents died when I was just a kid. I was raised in a series of foster homes until I turned eighteen. After I left the system, I drifted for a while, then joined the navy. Eventually, I ended up working in the intelligence community before I was recruited into a classified special ops program, code name Phoenix."

When he paused, Von Meter nodded encouragingly. "Please go on."

"The training was conducted in a series of underground bunkers at the old Montauk Air Force

Station on Long Island. I remember very little about my time there or the missions we carried out, but I do recall being on board a submarine at some point. There was an accident. Some kind of explosion. We crash-dove to the bottom of the North Atlantic where we were trapped for days. Most of the crew died. A hundred and something men. I think there were other survivors besides me, but I never saw them. I spent weeks in the hospital where I was subjected to long periods of isolation and rigorous debriefing sessions. After a while, I lost track of time and the details of the accident began to fade. Some days I had a hard time remembering my own name.'' He paused as the feelings of loneliness and confusion washed over him once again. Then he shrugged them away. ''That's about it. I was later discharged from the navy.''

''They said you were mentally unfit to serve.''

Zac got up and walked over to the window to stare out at the snow. The discharge still rankled five years later.

Von Meter spoke from behind him. ''You mentioned something about Project Phoenix. It was, and is, an operation much larger in scope than a special ops program.''

Zac turned from the window. Something the old man said rang a bell. ''How so?''

"Project Phoenix is a privately funded, covert organization comprised of scientists, military personnel, and leaders from business and technology—some of the finest minds in the world. The advances we've made in psychotronics, telekinetic studies and interdimensional phasing, just to name a few, are far more vast and intricate than most people could even begin to imagine."

Zac wondered if he was dealing with a lucid mind here. The things the old man spoke of were impossible. And yet…something inside him warned that Von Meter spoke the truth. And that truth was somehow directly related to Zac. That was why he was here.

He studied the old man for a moment, trying to gauge his sanity. "Even if what you say is true, what does any of that have to do with me?"

"The goal of Project Phoenix was to create an army of secret warriors—super soldiers if you will—with psionic abilities. Once their training was complete, their memories were erased and they were sent back home or back out into society until such time as they were needed. That's why you're here, Zac. You are being called back into service."

"Wait a minute." Zac's pulse jumped in spite of himself. "Are you saying I'm one of these…super soldiers?" When the old man nodded, Zac laughed, but the sound seemed hollow even to him. "Obviously, you've got the wrong man, doc. If I had any special abilities, psionic or otherwise, I wouldn't be working in a dump like Blue Monday's. And I sure as hell wouldn't be here."

"But you do possess a special skill," Von Meter assured him. "One that makes you uniquely qualified for the mission on which you are about to embark."

"Mission? Uh, no. I don't think so. Sorry, old man. I don't take orders anymore, not from you or anyone else. And even if I did, you haven't said one single thing to convince me you aren't running some kind of con here. My guess is you need a patsy, but I'm not as desperate or as stupid as you seem to think. And, as far as this mission of yours is concerned, I'm not going anywhere but home."

He started to rise, but Von Meter's gruff voice halted him. "Wait. Just hear me out a moment longer. If you still want to leave after I'm finished, then you can do so with my blessing."

Zac didn't really care whether he had the old man's blessing or not, but seeing as how he didn't have anywhere else to go on a cold, blustery night in Philadelphia, he sat back down. If nothing else, Von Meter's charade could get interesting.

"Have you ever heard of something called the Philadelphia Experiment?"

Zac nodded. "Yeah. It's a bar on South Street."

The old man waved an impatient hand. "I'm not talking about a bar. I'm talking about an event. The disappearance of a U.S. warship back in 1943."

Zac eyed the old man with skepticism. "I know what you're talking about. But the Philadelphia Experiment is a myth. An urban legend based on the navy's experiments during the war with electromagnetic fields. Scientists were trying to find a way to make ships invisible to enemy mines by demagnetizing the hulls, but according to the legend, what they achieved instead was visual stealth. Optical invisibility. Whatever you want to call it. That sound about right?"

Von Meter nodded eagerly. "Yes, precisely. But what if I were to tell you that the Philadelphia Experiment is more than a legend?" He leaned forward, his eyes lit with an uncanny glow. "What if I were to tell you that the powerful magnetic fields created by the specially designed generators installed on that ship somehow ripped a hole in the space-time continuum? What if I were to tell you the ship didn't become invisible? It entered another dimension. It traveled forward in time, and when it came back, it left something in its wake."

Tingles stole up and down Zac's spine as he gazed at Von Meter. "What are you talking about?"

"I'm talking about a secret passage. A time tunnel, if you will. A wormhole that links the present to the past. To 1943 to be precise." The old man's smile deepened Zac's chill. "We've found it, you see. We know the location of the wormhole, and we have every intention of sending someone through it. Someone who is uniquely qualified for such a mission. That someone...is you, Zac."

Chapter Two

She dreamed that Adam was still alive. The vision seemed so real, it was as if that day in the park had never happened.

But even in her sleep, Camille knew it *wasn't* real. Adam was dead, and no amount of wishful thinking was ever going to bring him back.

But his voice… She could still hear it in her sleep.

"Mom, can you really teach me how to play baseball?" he was asking her.

In her dream, Camille grinned down at him, her heart swelling with love. "You bet I can. I'll teach you just like my mother taught me."

"Why didn't your dad teach you?"

"Because my dad died when I was little. You know that, Adam. We've talked about it before."

"Did my dad die, too?" he asked solemnly. "Is that why he's not here to play baseball with me?"

How was she supposed to answer that question, Camille wondered sadly, when the truth was something she still hadn't come to terms with herself? Adam's father wasn't dead. He simply...didn't remember them.

Luckily, the child suddenly became distracted by something else, and he let the matter drop. "Mom, why is that man watching us?"

Startled, she glanced up. "What man?"

"That man over there." Adam was holding her hand, and his grasp tightened almost imperceptibly, as if he somehow sensed danger.

Camille followed her son's gaze. About thirty feet from the path, a man stood in the shade of an elm tree. Sunglasses obscured his eyes, but she could tell that he was staring at them.

A chill ran up her spine. There was something...unnerving about the way he watched them. As if...he knew them.

Camille was certain she'd never seen *him* before. She would have remembered. He had a striking appearance, the kind you didn't forget. Dressed all in black, he was tall and thin, with silvery-blond hair combed straight back from his face.

Camille shivered again. She and Adam had purposely drifted away from the more populated area of the park so that they would have plenty of room to play pitch without worrying about stray balls hitting toddlers. She suddenly found herself wishing they hadn't wandered quite so far away from the swing sets, jungle gyms and mothers pushing babies in strollers.

"Adam, maybe we should go back—"

"No, Mom, please." He squinted up at her. "You promised you'd teach me today. Can't we just stay for a little while? Please? Pretty please?"

It wasn't in her son's nature to remain obstinate for long. If they left now, he'd soon get over his disappointment. He was an easygoing child. Loving and affectionate although, like his father, he had a bit of devilment lurking in those dark, soulful eyes. Eyes that could melt her heart with just once glance. And when he gave her that look—as he was now—she didn't stand a chance.

"Okay, just a few pitches," Camille relented, her gaze moving back to the stranger. Surely he meant them no harm. They were still within shouting distance of the playground, and they were visible from the street. It was broad daylight, a beautiful summer's afternoon. What could possibly happen?

She spent a few minutes showing Adam how to hold the ball. "Your hands are too small now to grip across the seams, but we'll work on that as you get older. Right now, just try to get the ball out on your fingertips. See? Like this.'' She demonstrated the technique. ''And keep your wrist loose and cocked back. That way you can use it as part of your throwing motion.''

After a few more minutes of instruction, she backed up and tossed Adam the ball. ''Now, throw it to me, son. Just like I showed you.''

After a few tries, he was able to get the ball to her with some accuracy and catch it when she threw it back.

''I did it, Mom! Did you see me?'' He jumped up and down in his excitement.

''Good job! I knew you'd be a natural!''

It was true. He'd inherited his father's athletic prowess along with his dark good looks and innate charisma. Someday he'd be a real heartbreaker. Just like his father.

They played for several more minutes. Camille was just about to suggest they head back to the car when her last pitch got away from Adam. The sound of his laughter echoed back to her as he chased after the ball. She laughed, too, at first, enjoying the moment, but then suddenly her breath quickened in alarm.

Something was wrong.

The grass should have slowed the ball's momentum, but instead it kept rolling and rolling, always just out of Adam's reach. She heard him laugh again as he tried to chase it down.

She must have thrown the ball harder than she meant to. That had to be it....

"Adam! Wait! Let me get the ball. Adam!"

Out of the corner of her eye, Camille spotted the stranger again. He'd moved into the sun, and now she could see him more clearly. As she watched, he slowly reached up and removed his dark glasses. Camille gasped. There was something odd about his eyes....

A fist of terror closed around her heart. He meant to harm them. She knew that without a doubt. She had to get to Adam. She had to protect him....

But the harder she tried to catch him, the farther away he seemed.

He was almost to the street by now, still chasing the ball. Try as she might, she couldn't reach him.

"Adam!" She screamed his name, but a sudden gust of wind tore it away. "Adam!"

The ball rolled into the middle of the street and stopped. Without hesitation, Adam darted after it. He was so focused on the ball that he didn't see the blue sedan roaring down the street toward him....

CAMILLE AWAKENED with her dead son's name on her lips and tears drying on her face. She thought at first the pounding in her head was the echo of her own heartbeat, but then she realized someone was banging on her front door.

Lifting her head, she squinted at the clock. Just after seven. Had she overslept?

Her gaze darted to the window where she could see the sun slipping below the edge of a distant ridge. She sank back in relief. It was evening, not morning. She must have dozed off while listening to the news. The radio was still on, and she could hear the transmission fading in and out. She reached over and snapped off the old Motorola, but it took a moment for the static to die away.

The pounding came again, more desperate this time, and someone shouted her name. She put a hand to her eyes, trying to wipe away the last of the sleep as she swung her legs to the floor. Running a hand through her messy hair, she got up and hurried to the front door.

The dream was still so fresh in her head that when she glanced through the sidelight and saw the little boy standing on her front porch, her initial instinct was to throw open the door and sweep him into her arms, even though she almost immediately recognized him as one of the Clutter children from down the road. He didn't even resemble Adam. Her son had been dark haired while Billy was a freckle-faced redhead.

Camille drew back the door and scowled down at the child. "Billy? What's all the commotion about? Is everything okay—"

He grabbed her hand and tugged. "You gotta come, Miss Camille. Davy says you gotta come *right now*—"

"Whoa, wait a minute. Come where?" Camille felt as if only half her pistons were firing while Billy operated at full throttle. She had a hard time keeping up.

"You gotta come to the mine!" His voice rose in agitation. "Davy says—"

"To the *mine?* You mean the old deserted coal mine up on the ridge? You boys didn't go up there, did you? That place is dangerous—" Camille sank to her knees and gripped the boy's shoulders. "Billy, tell me what happened. Is someone hurt?" When he nodded, her stomach lurched. "Who's hurt? One of the twins? Donny?"

He shook his head, gulping in air as he tried to catch his breath. "No, not Donny. Not Davy, either. It's a man. We found him in the mine. He's croaked and everything, and Davy says he's a German spy probably!"

Camille tried to keep her voice even, tried not to

let her own panic show in her actions, but she saw Billy wince as her grip tightened on his arms. With an effort, she released him. "Are you sure he's dead?"

The boy nodded vigorously. "Yes, ma'am, he's real dead. Davy said to come get you on account of our pop's not home and you'd know what to do."

Camille wasn't so sure about that. "Where is your father?"

"He's at work. He won't be home until real late probably."

Daniel Clutter, a widower, was employed as an engineer at one of the city's secret facilities, and his work kept him on the reservation for long, exhausting hours at a time. He'd recently hired a full-time housekeeper to watch the boys in his absence, but the woman had to be over sixty and was no match for a precocious seven-year-old, let alone his twelve-year-old twin brothers, who were almost always up to mischief. Davy, the self-appointed ringleader, was cunning and clever and utterly fearless. A dangerous combination, in Camille's estimation.

And now it appeared that he'd led his brothers inside a deserted mine. He had no idea of the danger they could have encountered. A dead German spy was the least of it.

So what was she supposed to do? The cottage didn't have a telephone and the road back to the mine was overgrown and impassable. She'd have to go on foot.

"Here's what I want you to do," she told the still-excited child. She put a hand beneath his chin. "Listen carefully. I want you to go straight home and tell Mrs. Fowler I've gone up on the ridge looking for the twins. I'll bring them home as soon as I find them. Understand?"

The little boy swallowed. "Yes, ma'am, but Davy said I wasn't to tell anybody but you. He said—"

"Never mind what your brother said." Camille lowered her voice to a stern, no-nonsense tone, the kind she'd once used to let Adam know she meant business. "You do as I tell you and maybe, just maybe, I can keep you boys out of trouble."

Camille turned him toward the front porch and gave him a swat on his behind. "Hurry, now. Tell Mrs. Fowler you're both to stay put until you hear from me."

As the boy shot across the front porch, Camille whirled. Hurrying through the silent house, she grabbed first-aid supplies from the bathroom and stuffed them into a bag, along with a flashlight and her .45. Two minutes later, she was out the door.

A path behind the cottage led into the woods, but the trail ended after a half mile or so and the terrain soon became rough and overgrown. Darkness was falling, too, but Camille didn't turn on her flashlight. Batteries were hard to come by, and she'd learned to use them—and a lot of other things—sparingly. But in another few minutes, the last rays of the sunset would fade and the topography would become even more treacherous.

At least she knew the area. Camille had made it a priority to familiarize herself with every square inch of the surrounding countryside. She'd found all the hiding places and the discreet trails across the ridge that led straight to the city. From one of those hidden vantages, she'd memorized the rotation of the guards, the weaknesses in the city's defenses, and she knew better than anyone how easily a spy or saboteur—or even an assassin—could slip in and out undetected.

Breathing heavily, she emerged into a clearing on the face of the ridge and immediately spotted one of the twins pacing in front of the old mine shaft. The entrance had been boarded up at one time, but some of the planks had been pried loose and the rest were broken. The fresh splintering of the wood suggested that someone had come in and out of the mine recently.

Camille hurried over to the boy, noticing in the fading light the scar above his right eyebrow which told her this was the more docile twin, Donny.

"Where's Davy?" she asked anxiously.

Donny nodded toward the mine. "In there." He reached for a lantern hooked on a peg just outside the entrance. "Come on, I'll show you."

"No, I'll go in alone," Camille said quickly. "You wait out here."

"But Davy said—"

"I don't give a damn what Davy said." Camille knew her voice sounded harsh, but she didn't care. She had to somehow make the boys realize how dangerous the mine was. She had to make sure they didn't come back here. "Do you have any idea how foolish it was for you boys to come up here? Let alone dragging poor Billy along with you? It could be one of you lying dead in there."

She waved a hand toward the mine entrance. "This place has been abandoned for years. The supports are all rotting. What if there'd been a cave-in? What if you'd gotten trapped inside? No one would have known where to find you. You could have been buried alive and no one would have ever known what happened to you."

Donny's eyes widened as he listened to her. Good, Camille thought. Maybe she was getting through to him. Maybe if she scared him enough, he'd keep his brothers away from this place.

"Now—" she reached inside the bag for her flashlight "—I'm going in there to find your brother and then I want you both to go straight home and never come back here again. You understand me?"

Donny gulped and nodded. "Yes, ma'am."

"Good." She brushed past him to the entrance, pausing just inside to flick on the flashlight and shine the beam around the room.

The evening was hot and muggy, but inside the mine the temperature was a good ten degrees cooler. Shivering in the gloom, Camille glanced over her shoulder. Donny watched her anxiously from the entrance. When he saw her looking at him, he jumped back.

"Which way?" she asked.

Tentatively, he stepped back up to the entrance. "See that tunnel over there? When it forks, go right. That's where Davy is."

The series of tunnels had been dug horizontally into the hillside. The passage Camille took was narrow and, except for the beam of her flashlight, pitch-black. Thankful she wasn't claustrophobic, she followed the metal rails that had once been used to transport loads of coal from the mine. As she approached the fork, she could hear water dripping somewhere nearby and the more ominous sound of the ancient log braces creaking beneath their weight.

"Davy?"

"In here," came the soft reply.

The opening lay to her right, and, as Camille ducked through, she gasped in shock.

The dead man lay sprawled on the dirt floor, his face and clothing covered in blood and grime. The stench of unwashed flesh permeated the air, and Camille had to press her hand to her mouth to keep from gagging.

Davy Clutter, evidently unperturbed by either the smell or the sight of all that blood, squatted on the ground beside the corpse. He'd hung a lantern nearby, and the flickering light cast wild shadows across the walls and gave the boy a strange, demonic appearance.

He had a stick in one hand that he'd been using to draw pictures in the dirt while he waited for Camille. When he heard her gasp, he looked up, his eyes glowing eerily in the lamplight.

"Davy? Are you okay?"

"Yes, ma'am." He rose to his feet. "But he's not. Someone killed him."

"How do you know?"

"His head's bashed in."

"Maybe he fell and hit his head on a rock." Camille's gaze slid reluctantly back to the still form on the ground. "Are you sure he's dead?"

Davy poked the body with his stick. When there was no response, he shrugged and glanced up. "See?"

Camille tried not to be disturbed by the boy's cavalier attitude. In wartime, death was no stranger to anyone, even children. Davy was obviously handling the situation the best way he knew how. He'd convinced himself that the dead man was an enemy spy and therefore, unworthy of compassion.

Summoning her own resolve, Camille decided she'd better check for a pulse, but as she moved toward the body, an avalanche of dirt and gravel rained down in the tunnel behind her. She glanced over her shoulder, then whirled back to Davy. "We've got to get you out of here. This place isn't safe—"

A low rumble from somewhere nearby caused them both to jump. For the first time, Camille saw fear flash across the boy's features as he moved toward her. "What's that?"

"I think it's a cave-in somewhere back in the mine." Camille's heart started to pound as she grabbed the boy's hand. "Come on. We have to get out of here."

Davy glanced down at the dead man. ''What about him?''

''We'll have to leave him for now. There's nothing we can do for him anyway. Come on. We have to hurry!''

Camille propelled Davy to the opening and, once he'd scurried through, she started to follow. But a movement caught her eye, and slowly she turned back to the dead man.

His eyes were open. They hadn't been before.

Camille put a hand to her mouth. He was alive!

Another shower of dirt and rocks spewed into the tunnel, and Davy tugged on her hand. ''Come on!''

But Camille couldn't move. She couldn't tear her gaze from those eyes. Those dark, gleaming, seductive eyes.

The eyes of the man she'd been sent to kill.

Chapter Three

"Are you ready for me to continue?" Von Meter prodded.

"Why bother, old man? I've heard enough of your fairy tales for one night." Zac got up and walked back over to the window to watch the snow.

Von Meter's tone grew impatient. "You call it a fairy tale, and yet I've told you nothing but the truth. Why do you doubt me?"

Zac traced the outline of a snowflake on the frosty pane. "Call me a skeptic, but I have a tendency to believe only what I've witnessed with my own two eyes. And I know I've never seen anyone—how did you put it?—phase into another dimension. You show me someone who can walk through a wall, and then we'll talk."

"But you saw what Roth could do. You witnessed his telekinetic abilities with your own two eyes."

"A slamming door would be the easiest thing in the world to rig. Besides, you said it yourself. This place is old and drafty." Zac glanced around. "You've probably got doors banging shut right and left in here. You'll have to do a lot better than that to convince me you're sane, old man."

"You are being deliberately obtuse," Von Meter accused in exasperation. "You've seen all the things I've described. You've witnessed extraordinary phenomena that cannot even be imagined, let alone explained, in the ordinary world."

"And how convenient that I don't remember any of it," Zac said dryly.

Again Von Meter's tone grew edgy, as if he, a man of science, was unaccustomed to dealing with such a cynical mind. "It's true your memories were erased after the explosion. But I explained all that. It was a necessary precaution. Secrecy was, and is, of the utmost importance to Project Phoenix. We can't allow the narrow-minded meddlers of the world to destroy what we've worked so hard to achieve." He took a breath. "As for your memories...they will return in time. Some of them, at least. The ones you'll need to carry out your mission."

"There you go again." Zac remained unmoved by the strange old man's prediction. "I don't know *how I can make myself any clearer. I'm not in the service anymore, so I don't have to take orders from you or anyone else. I left all that behind me. I'm mentally unfit to serve, remember? So whatever this mission is you keep talking about, you'd better find yourself another guy. I'm not interested."*

"And yet you're still here," Von Meter observed.

Yes, he was still there, Zac thought angrily, but he had no idea why. Von Meter was obviously demented. Interdimensional phasing, telekinetic powers, time travel. Apparently in this crazy old man's universe, anything was possible.

And what about the woman? Zac wondered. The one who haunted his dreams. Did she reside somewhere in Von Meter's universe? Or had she ever really existed?

"I created her. I put her in your head. She was my gift to you."

Well, that answered his question, didn't it? Assuming he could believe anything Von Meter had told him. And that would be a pretty damn big assumption.

"There's still a lot more you need to know, and we're running out of time. Please allow me to finish," Von Meter urged.

Zac shrugged. "You can talk until you're blue in

the face, but my mind is made up. Whatever you're peddling, I'm not buying.''

''I guess we'll just have to see about that, won't we?'' Von Meter's smile seemed strained as he reached for a cigar in the humidor he kept on his desk. But rather than light up, he merely passed the tobacco beneath his nose, inhaled deeply, then returned the cigar to the box. ''The technology I've referred to—the interdimensional phasing, telekinesis, psychotronics—the root of all this extraordinary technology can be traced back to the experiment that was conducted on that ship more than sixty years ago.''

''The Philadelphia Experiment, you mean.''

The old man nodded. ''In World War II, the government was engaged in many classified programs, the most famous, of course, being the Manhattan Project. The development of the A-bomb was concentrated primarily in three secret locations: Hanford, Washington; Los Alamos, New Mexico; and Oak Ridge, Tennessee. Buried within the confines of Oak Ridge was another program known as Project Rainbow. It was run by a man named Nicholas Kessler—''

Zac turned. ''Kessler?''

''Does that name mean something to you?'' Von Meter asked carefully.

Zac studied the old man's features. "I'm not sure. Should it?"

"Perhaps you know him by reputation," Von Meter said, but his tone seemed evasive to Zac, as if he were deliberately withholding information. "Kessler was an internationally renowned physicist who had worked with the likes of Albert Einstein and Max Born before the war. He possessed one of the most brilliant minds of the time, but, unfortunately, his genius was tainted by his lack of courage and vision. He began to have serious doubts about the work he was doing for the government, and he tried his best to get the project shut down. But he was too late. The military had seen the possibilities such a new technology could offer. The war could conceivably be won, not in a matter of years or even months, but in days."

Zac stared at the old man. "You almost sound as if you really believe all this."

Von Meter's gaze admonished him. "Of course, I believe it. And soon you will, too."

"So you keep saying," Zac muttered.

"An experiment involving a U.S. warship was scheduled for August 15, 1943, despite Kessler's repeated warnings regarding the crew's safety. But the military overrode his objections. The sacrifice of one ship's crew, they reasoned, wasn't such a *high price to pay for the millions of lives that could be spared.''*

''The good of the many outweighs the needs of a few,'' Zac said.

''Precisely. But on the eve of the experiment, Dr. Kessler stole aboard the ship and tried to sabotage the generators used to produce the magnetic fields. He was apprehended before he could destroy them, and the experiment went on as planned the following day. When the generators were fired up, a strange, greenish glow enveloped the deck. The ship began to fade until only a faint outline remained. Then it disappeared altogether, only to reappear some five hours later in another green haze. It must have been the most amazing spectacle one could ever hope to witness,'' Von Meter said reverently.

''And the crew?''

He hesitated. *''There were problems just as Dr. Kessler had predicted.''*

''What kind of problems?''

''Several of the men became violently ill. The others were either dead or suffering from confusion and dementia. And at least one man was missing. Those who survived were eventually dismissed from the military as mentally unfit to serve.'' The old man nodded at Zac's quizzical look. *''Yes. Just as you were nearly sixty years later.''*

"Are you implying there's some kind of connection?" Zac asked doubtfully.

"I'm merely suggesting that there are no real coincidences in this world." The old man rubbed a hand across his eyes, as if he, too, were tiring of the conversation. *"After the experiment, Kessler was so appalled by the condition of the crew that he lobbied even harder to have the project shut down. He managed to convince a congressional oversight committee that the new technology not only had the power to change the world as we know it, but could challenge the very essence of humankind."*

"Was he right?"

"Yes. But Kessler refused to consider the possibility that the ultimate outcome of such an amazing science might be a better *human."* Von Meter shifted restlessly in his chair. *"Politicians have never been known for their vision, and this group was no exception. They agreed with Kessler and cut off funding for the project. Kessler even burned his own notes in the hopes that the experiment could never be repeated, but luckily some of them were saved and became the basis of Project Phoenix."*

"That's quite a story," Zac said. *"But aren't you forgetting something? You haven't explained the wormhole."*

"*Ah, yes, the wormhole.*" *Von Meter tented his fingers beneath his chin.* "*You see, a wormhole is an inherently unstable entity. When the ship rematerialized, the tunnel through which it had traveled should have collapsed once its power source was cut off. But Kessler did something to those generators that night. He damaged them in such a way that at least one of them couldn't be shut down properly. As a result, the wormhole was able to gather enough negative energy—exotic matter, we call it—to overcome the gravitational pull and stabilize.*"

"*Sounds like a lot of mumbo jumbo to me,*" *Zac said.*

"*I don't see why. The existence of wormholes has been theorized in quantum physics for decades, and the existence of this particular wormhole has been known by us for years. Until recently, however, we were unable to locate the entrance despite exhaustive searches. And, all the while, it was right under our noses.*" *The old man's boredom faded, replaced once again by a subtle excitement.*

"*And now that you've found it, you want to send me through it,*" *Zac said.* "*For what purpose?*"

"*To destroy it.*"

Zac's eyebrows shot up. "*Let me get this straight. You've looked for this thing for years, and now* when you've found it, you want me to destroy it? Why?''

"Because it's the only way," Von Meter said with heavy regret. "Think about the consequences of such a passageway. Someone from the present could travel back to 1943 and, using their knowledge of modern technology, literally change the course of history. The outcome of the war. Imagine a world in which the Allied forces had been vanquished.''

Zac grimaced.

"Now do you see why the wormhole must be destroyed?" Von Meter asked quietly.

"I get your point, old man. But assuming any of this is true, why not just find a way to close up the opening? Or…hide it somehow.''

"Even if that were possible, the risk would always exist that someone at some later date, some future generation, would discover it. We can't take that chance.''

"But if I go back in time, won't my very presence in 1943 change history?" Zac insisted.

Von Meter's expression turned grim. "That's why you must be extremely careful. You are being sent back to a very dangerous time. There will be those who would lure you into the intrigue of the day, but you must not get involved. There will be

temptations, but you must resist them. At any cost.
*Even the smallest interference could be disastrous.
Your mission is simple. You must prevent Dr. Kessler from tampering with those generators so that
once the ship rematerializes, they can be shut off,
thus triggering an event horizon. The wormhole will
collapse, but everything else must remain the same.
Is that understood?''*

*Zac walked over to Von Meter's desk and sat
down. ''Just for the sake of argument, let's assume
everything you've told me is true, and let's say I
agree to go back and make sure those generators
get turned off...what happens once the wormhole
collapses?''*

*Von Meter's gaze darkened. ''It's very possible
that you will be trapped in 1943.''*

*Zac gave a little laugh. ''I can see why you don't
exactly have volunteers lining up outside your
door.''*

*''To get back to your own time, you must reenter
the wormhole before the ship rematerializes. The
logistics of the mission will make this extremely difficult...unless...''*

*''That had better be a pretty damn big 'unless',''
Zac warned.*

*''Unless you can recruit someone from the past,
someone you trust to help you.''*

"You have someone in mind?"

Something flickered in Von Meter's eyes, a shadow Zac couldn't quite decipher. *"Nicholas Kessler himself."*

"And just what makes you think he'd be willing to help me?" Zac demanded. *"Or even listen to me? And come to think of it, why am I still listening to you? For all I know, you're just some nutcase who escaped from a nearby asylum."*

Ignoring the sarcasm once again, Von Meter opened a drawer in his desk and withdrew a gold chain from which a tiny medallion dangled. He held it out and Zac reluctantly took it. *"What is this?"*

"It was given to Kessler by a young woman he knew before he left Germany. She later died in a concentration camp. She had it specially cast for him in her father's jewelry shop in Berlin. It's one of a kind."

"How did you happen across it?" Zac asked suspiciously. He held up the chain, and the gold ignited in the lamplight, sparking a feeling of déjà vu deep inside him. He'd seen this medallion before. Somewhere, at some time, he'd held it in his hand....

A shiver ran up his spine as he lifted his gaze to Von Meter's. *"Where did you get this?"* he asked again.

"It doesn't matter how it came to be in my possession," the old man said evasively. *"The only thing that matters is its usefulness to you."*

"What do you mean?"

"That medallion will convince Nicholas Kessler to help you."

"How?"

"You must trust me on that."

Zac's fist closed around the chain. *"Why should I trust you about any of this?"*

"Because you have no choice."

"No choice?" Zac rose. *"Think again, old man. There's always a choice."* He turned toward the door.

"You can go," Von Meter called softly behind him. *"But you'll come back, just as you were compelled to come here earlier. Just as you were compelled to return when you walked out the first time. And do you know why? Because a part of you already knows that I'm telling you the truth. You are a super soldier, Zac. A Phoenix warrior trained and programmed to go to extraordinary lengths to carry out a mission. You have no choice because that is who you are. That is what you are."*

Zac whirled, his gaze contemptuous. But even as the rage slowly built inside him, he felt something *else stir to life as well. Excitement. Adrenaline. The thrill of the hunt.*

And deeper still, the awakening of senses he hadn't even known he possessed.

THE DREAM FADED. Von Meter disappeared and Zac was left drifting in darkness. He had a vague sense of having been injured, of being cared for. He could feel gentle hands on him from time to time, but he couldn't wake up. He seemed to be trapped in some shadowy netherworld where dreams and reality were one.

She was there. The woman who had haunted his sleep for so long.

He knew her intimately by now. Her touch, her kiss. The feel of her pale, silky skin beneath his hands.

Her voice was like a siren's song. The soothing tones had the power to lead him from the darkness. Or lure him more deeply into it.

He could hear that voice now, soft, lyrical, beguiling. "I knew you'd come," she said. "It was just a matter of time."

She laughed, a hard, brittle sound that seemed to pierce Zac's soul. "But then, time is such a relative concept, isn't it?"

She was silent for a moment, and, when she

spoke again, the bitterness had faded. "What happened to you? Who did this to you? Who would want to kill you…besides me?"

Another silence. "I don't think I can go through with it," she whispered. "I know how much is at stake, and yet when I saw you lying there…when I thought you were dead…"

For just a split second, Zac could have sworn he felt her hand on his face, the brush of her lips against his. It was almost enough to make him leave the darkness behind.

Almost…but not quite. Not yet.

She sniffed, as if fighting back tears. "Why did you come? Why did Grandfather have to be right? Why did it have to be you?"

She paused again, and, in the ensuing quiet, Zac could hear the pounding of her heart. Or was that his own?

"I can't let any of that matter, though, can I?" she said harshly. "I have a job to do. I have to find out why you're here so for now I need you alive. You can't die on me, Zac. Do you hear me? You can't die…not knowing about Adam."

ZAC KNEW HE'D SEEN *the boy before. There was something touchingly familiar about that solemn little face and those dark, innocent eyes.*

He had a baseball in one hand and a glove in the other, and it seemed to Zac that the child was bathed in light. A brilliant, white light that warmed Zac all the way to his soul.

"Hey, mister, you wanna play some catch?" the boy asked hopefully.

Zac shrugged. "Sure. Baseball's my favorite sport."

The boy squinted up at him. "You any good at it?"

"Not too shabby." Zac backed up a few paces and squatted. "Okay, kid, show me what you got."

The boy wound up and let one rip, a perfect strike over the invisible home plate. Zac shook his hand as if the ball had stung his palm. "Hey, kid, where'd you learn to throw like that?"

"My mom taught me."

"Your mom, huh?" Zac rose and glanced around. "Where is she?"

"She's waiting for you."

"Waiting for me? What do you mean?"

The boy walked slowly toward him, his eyes dark and mesmerizing. "It's getting late, mister. You better go."

"Go where?" Suddenly, Zac realized he didn't have a clue where he was or what he was supposed to do. He'd never felt so lost in his life.

The boy walked right up to him and gave him a push. "You gotta go, okay? It's time...."

"YOU'RE SUPPOSED TO BE DEAD, Mr. Riley," an angry voice said in his ear.

That voice pulled Zac from the dream, from the boy. He struggled against it for a moment, but he was too weak to resist.

The voice drew even closer to his ear. "What were you doing in that mine shaft? Who sent you here? The FBI? The OSS? It doesn't matter. The military must not be allowed to finish what they've started behind that fence. Your interference will not be tolerated—"

"What do you think you're doing?" a second voice suddenly demanded.

Zac sensed another presence as someone hustled into the room.

The first visitor seemed stunned into silence for a moment, then said calmly, "I was just fluffing his pillow."

"Fluffing his pillow?" the second voice repeated doubtfully. "For a minute there, I thought..."

"What did you think?"

She gave a nervous laugh. "It looked as if you were trying to smother the poor man."

The first visitor laughed, too. "Smother him? Now that's a good one."

"I must be working too hard. I'm so tired I'm starting to see things." They both laughed again, but something lingered in the second voice that might have been suspicion.

"Looks like you're here to take his temperature, and I've got things to do myself so I'll just get out of your way," the first voice offered.

"I don't mean to run you off."

"No, that's fine. I'll come back later." A hand patted Zac's shoulder. "You can count on that."

"DON'T YOU HAVE TO GO HOME?" Zac asked.

"I can't go until you do," the boy said.

Zac glanced down in confusion. "Why?"

The boy shrugged. "You might not be able to find your way without me." He took Zac's hand. "Come on. I'll walk you part of the way."

"Shouldn't it be the other way around?" Zac asked in amusement. "Shouldn't I walk you home?"

"You can't."

"Why not?"

The boy paused. "Because that's not the way it works."

He was a very strange little boy. And yet there

*was something infinitely appealing about him. Zac
found he didn't want to leave him. He knelt and put
his hands on the boy's shoulders. "Do I know you?
I don't think we've ever met, but...you seem familiar to me."*

*The boy's dark eyes glinted, and he turned away
suddenly, wiping a quick hand across his nose.
"We gotta go, okay? It'll be dark soon."*

*"Tell me your name first," Zac said. "And then
I'll go with you."*

*But it was too late. The little boy had already left
without him, and Zac had never felt so alone.*

"How is he today, Doctor?"

Zac heard the soft voice as if from a great distance.

"He seems to be slipping away. Pulse is weak,
blood pressure dropping... It's only a matter of
time, I'm afraid."

"Poor thing. It's such a shame. He's really quite
handsome, isn't he?"

"I wouldn't know about that, Nurse. And, in the
future, I suggest that you spend more time tending
to the patient's needs than in nurturing your own
romantic fantasies about him."

"Yes, Doctor."

HE LOOKED TERRIBLE. Even devoid of the grime and blood from the mine, his face was so drawn and blanched that Camille barely recognized him.

He'd once been the most virile and handsome man she'd ever known, and it hurt her now to see him like this. So pale and still. So near death…

"I can't go through this again," she whispered raggedly. "I *can't*…."

And yet even in her anguish, she recognized the irony of her pain. He was the enemy now. She couldn't let that fact slip away from her, even for a second.

She tried to harden her heart as she gazed down at him, but instead of hatred and contempt, she felt an irresistible desire to press her lips against his mouth and breathe her own life into his lungs.

"WHY'D YOU COME BACK?" Zac asked the boy. He seemed to have appeared from nowhere, and Zac felt an overwhelming sense of relief. He ruffled the child's hair in affection.

The boy drew away from him. "You have to go, mister."

"My name is Zac."

"You have to go…Zac."

"You keep saying that, but there's nowhere I need to be. I'd rather just stay here with you. We

could go to a baseball game or something. Would you like that?''

The little boy shook his head, but his eyes glistened with something that tore at Zac's heart. That made him long for something he hadn't even known he'd lost.

"We could play catch," he suggested hopefully. "Just for a little while."

The boy shook his head again. "You have to go."

"Please…" But Zac didn't even understand his own plea. He just knew that when he left, he'd never see the boy again, and the pain of that knowledge was almost more than he could bear. "I can't leave you," he whispered.

The little boy lifted his hand and pointed behind Zac. He turned.

And there she was, still cloaked in mist. Still as elusive as ever.

"She's waiting for you," the boy said.

"But she's not real," Zac protested.

"She needs you. You have to help her."

"Help her do what?"

The boy began to back away.

"No, don't go," Zac begged.

"I have to."

"Not yet. Please. Just a little while longer."

"She needs you," the boy said. "You have to go to her. You have to help her."

Zac glanced back at the woman. He couldn't see her face clearly—he never could—but he felt her presence. He felt another presence, too. A danger that lurked deep within the shadows. She seemed to sense it, too. She lifted a hand in supplication, and Zac suddenly had the strongest urge to rush to her, to take her in his arms and never let her go.

An unaccountable sorrow swept over him as he turned back to the boy. He had to make a choice. "I think I understand now. I have to go."

The child nodded and continued to slip away.

"Wait!" Zac put out a hand to stop him. "Please. Just tell me your name."

The little boy hesitated. "It's Adam," he said. "My name is Adam."

And then he was gone....

Chapter Four

"He moved his fingers!"

"It was probably just a muscle twitch." The taller of the two nurses put a hand to her mouth to smother a yawn.

"No, I saw it move," the blond nurse insisted. "And look at his eyes, Viv. The lids are fluttering. I think he's coming out of it!"

Camille had just walked into the ward, and now she paused, her heart pounding, as she listened to the nurses discuss Zac's condition. Was it true? Was he finally waking up from the coma?

It had been so long. Nearly a week since she and Davy had pulled him from that mine. She'd almost given up hope....

Camille closed her eyes, wanting nothing more than to succumb to the rush of emotions that threatened to engulf her, but she knew she had to fight the temptation. She couldn't allow herself to be pulled back into Zac Riley's universe. It hadn't worked the first time, and it wouldn't work now. It couldn't.

What she had to do instead was carry out her own mission. Too much rode on her success.

"I'll go fetch the doctor." The tall, redheaded nurse started to hurry off, but the other one caught her arm.

"Viv, wait! Look! He's trying to say something!"

"Can you understand him? What's he saying?"

Almost against her will, Camille took a step closer to Zac's bed. She could see his lips move frantically, but she couldn't hear him.

"There, there," the blond nurse soothed. "Try to stay calm—"

With surprising strength, Zac grabbed her arm and pulled her toward him. The nurse bent over him, listening intently.

"Can you make out what he's saying?" the tall nurse asked anxiously.

"I'm not sure. It sounds like a name. He keeps saying it over and over."

"What name?"

"Adam. I think he's asking for someone named Adam."

Camille's knees buckled as she reached blindly for the wall.

"COME ON, NOW. TIME TO WAKE UP."

The deep, no-nonsense voice penetrated Zac's dreamworld, but he was too weak and tired to respond. He wanted to bury himself in the darkness, but the voice was having none of that.

"Come on, wake up. You can do it. That's it. Keep fighting...."

Zac opened his eyes, batting his lids against the sudden brilliance. The light hurt. He wanted to close his eyes and sink back into the darkness, but it was too late. He was awake now, and there was no going back.

Three anxious faces peered down at him.

"Where am I?" he croaked.

"You're in County Hospital," the man told him. "I'm Dr. Cullen. This is Nurse Wilson and Nurse Brody. They've been taking very good care of you."

The shorter nurse, a blonde with blue eyes and deep dimples, beamed down at him. "We've all been very worried about you."

The other nurse, a tall, slender redhead, nodded

in agreement. "Indeed we have. Everyone will be so happy to hear that you're back with us."

Zac glanced at his surroundings in confusion. "What am I doing here?"

"You have a head injury," the doctor told him. "You've been unconscious for nearly a week."

"A week?" Panic welled inside Zac. He had someplace to go…something he had to do….

"Can you tell us your name?" the doctor urged gently.

He thought for a moment. "Zac…Riley."

The doctor nodded in satisfaction. "That's the name we found in your wallet. Do you remember anything about the accident?"

Accident? What accident? Zac shook his head.

"You were found in a deserted coal mine," the doctor explained. "We think you may have been injured in a cave-in, but that's only speculation on our part. I suspect everything will come back to you shortly, and you can fill us in on the details."

A coal mine? What the hell was going on here? What were these people talking about?

Zac's gaze flickered over them. There was something odd about their appearance. The women wore old-fashioned nurses' caps for one thing and their uniforms were long-sleeved and starchy white even though the temperature inside the hospital seemed quite hot.

Their hairstyles were different, too, as was the cut of the doctor's suit. They might have all been bit players in an old black-and-white movie.

And then a flood of memories came rushing back to Zac. *"We've found a wormhole. A time tunnel, if you will. A secret passage that links the present with the past. To 1943 to be precise."*

"What's the date?" he blurted. He tried to sit up, but, instantly, the doctor's hands were on his shoulders, pushing him firmly back against the pillow.

"Try to stay calm," he advised. "You've been through quite an ordeal, Mr. Riley. It'll take some time to get oriented—"

Zac grabbed his arm. "The date. What is the date?"

"It's the seventh day of August."

"And the year?"

The two nurses exchanged a glance before one of them said, "Nineteen forty-three."

Zac fell back against the pillow. "It's not too late then. I'm not too late."

"Too late for what?" the blond nurse asked him.

"To save the future," Zac muttered as he felt consciousness slipping away.

He heard the nurse giggle, and just before the

darkness claimed him again, Zac could have sworn he saw the doctor's eyes narrow in suspicion.

THE NURSES FAWNED OVER HIM incessantly. It was almost as if they were in a contest to see which one could lavish him with the most attention.

Zac supposed he should have been flattered, but he suspected their clucking had more to do with the lack of eligible men during wartime than it did with his own personal charisma. But he appreciated their concern just the same, especially considering that the hospital was so severely understaffed. He'd heard the nurses chattering about how some of the more experienced personnel had recently been lured to the hospital in Oak Ridge, leaving the county facility in dire straits. The remaining staff often saw their shifts doubled, sometimes tripled, but some-how the nurses always found the time to stop by Zac's bed as they made their rounds.

Dr. Cullen had also taken a keen interest in Zac's progress. He seemed amazed and truly baffled by how rapidly Zac appeared to be healing after having been unconscious for nearly a week. Zac gathered from some of the nurses' offhand comments that the doctor had all but given him up for dead. Then suddenly Zac had "awakened," apparently no worse for the wear. His vital signs and reflexes were normal, and he'd experienced nothing more than minor headaches and temporary blurred vision from the whole ordeal. A miracle recovery, they were calling it.

"The doctor says he's discharging you soon," Betty, the blond nurse, informed him. Her blue eyes sparkled in the sunlight streaming through a window at the end of the ward. "What are your plans when you leave here?"

Zac shrugged. "I guess I'll need to find a job and a place to live."

"You really shouldn't go back to work until you're fully recovered," she scolded. "And in the meantime, maybe I can help you find a place to stay, at least temporarily. I'll talk to my uncle. My cousin Tom is in the Pacific with the 25th Infantry. He was at Guadalcanal," she said proudly. "You can probably use his room for a little while."

"I wouldn't want to put anyone out," Zac hedged. Besides, he needed a place where he could come and go at all hours, without arousing suspicion.

"You wouldn't. Uncle Herbert would probably enjoy the company. He's been pretty lonely with Tommy away. And anyway there isn't another room to be had around here. Even the boarding houses and apartments in Knoxville are full. Some people have even rented out their chicken coops.'' She gave a delicate shudder. ''We're not exactly used to living high on the hog in these parts, but it would take somebody mighty desperate to bunk down in a henhouse. Although, I've seen some of those places behind the fence. Hutments, they call them. They're little more than boxes—''

''Betty Lou, are you talking the poor man's ear off *again?*'' Vivian, the redhead, demanded as she strode up to the bed.

''We were just trying to figure out a place for Mr. Riley…Zac—'' Betty dimpled sweetly ''—to stay when he's released.''

''No need to worry about that. I've already spoken to Mama.'' Vivian gave her friend a smug look. ''It's all set. He can stay with us.''

Betty looked aghast. ''And just where is he going to sleep? Both your bedrooms are three kids deep. Don't tell me you're going to put him in with Junior. That baby howls louder than a flea-bitten hound dog—''

''Well, it would beat listening to your uncle go on and on about the shrapnel he took in certain…delicate areas during the Great War,'' Vivian shot back. ''And did I hear correctly? Were you actually suggesting Mr. Riley sleep in a *chicken coop?*''

''I bet he'd rather sleep with the chickens than

put up with all those brats at your house," Betty muttered.

"Actually, I have a spare room," a female voice said from the doorway. "It's nothing fancy, but I can guarantee you some peace and quiet."

She was framed by so much light that Zac couldn't see her features at first. He assumed she was another nurse. Then she walked over to the end of his bed, and he caught his breath. She was the most striking woman he'd ever seen. Tall, slender, with dark hair and gorgeous eyes set off by the blue dress she wore. The garment was simply cut, but the straight skirt and fitted waist displayed curves that were soft and enticing. Her sleek hair was parted on the side and fell forward against her cheek before pooling on shapely shoulders.

There was something strangely familiar about her features, and yet, for the life of him, Zac couldn't place her. How in the hell could he have forgotten a woman like her?

As their gazes met, his heart tightened with an emotion he didn't understand.

"Do I know you?" he asked uncertainly.

She moved to his bedside. The nurses seemed to instinctively realize the newcomer had captured his undivided attention, and they backed off, but not without a measure of resentment.

Zac barely noticed. He had eyes for only one woman.

"Do I know you?" he asked again.

She tugged at a small gold locket she wore around her neck. The light shimmered off the chain, reminding him of the medallion Von Meter had given to him. Zac hoped it was still there, hidden away where he'd left it in the mine.

"My name is Camille Somersby. I'm the one who dragged you from the mine. Although I can't take all the credit. I had some help from my neighbor's sons. They're the ones who found you."

Zac frowned. Something she said tugged at a memory, but the image seemed to hover in the shadows, just out of his reach.

"I suppose I owe them, and you, my life," he muttered.

"Yes, I suppose you do." There was something strangely reluctant about her demeanor, as if she'd come here not of her own accord but of a necessity she couldn't quite bring herself to acknowledge. "So," she said briskly. "Have you remembered what you were doing in that mine in the first place?"

He shook his head. "Not really. I know I came here looking for a job on the reservation. I've had some experience in construction, and I'd heard they were hiring.''

''Some of the nurses seem to think that you must have heard about the mine in town, and, when you couldn't find a place to stay, you decided to go up there and camp out. Does that ring any bells?''

''It's all still a haze, I'm afraid.'' Zac decided it was time to change the subject. ''Speaking of a place to stay, you mentioned something about a room for rent?''

''Yes. I have a spare room. As you must have discovered, living arrangements have become something of a problem around here. I don't know how much you know about Oak Ridge....''

''Enough to know that whatever the military is doing behind that fence is causing a lot of resentment in the folks around here.''

''Yes, well, whatever goes on behind the fence stays there,'' she said. ''We're not allowed to talk about it.''

''We?''

''I work at one of the plants.'' She glanced around the ward, as if to make sure no one had overheard her. ''So, what do you say? Do we have a deal?'' When he hesitated, she said quickly, ''If it's the rent you're worried about, don't be. There's a lot to do around the cottage. A leaky roof and such. I'm sure you'll be able to earn your keep until you find a job. Maybe I could even speak to someone for you.''

He gave her a wary smile. ''You're being awfully generous to someone you don't even know. If I were the suspicious type, I might wonder why.''

''There's nothing mysterious about it,'' she said, but the nervous flutter of her hand as she reached for her locket told him something else. ''I have a vested interest in your welfare. I helped save your life, remember?'' She smiled, but something in her eyes, a lingering dusk, led Zac to believe that Camille Somersby was a woman with secrets. Dangerous secrets.

Every warning bell in his head clanged an alarm, but still he couldn't tear his gaze away. ''I can't help thinking we've met before,'' he murmured, his gaze tracing her features.

''In another time maybe,'' she said lightly. She twisted the locket around her finger. ''If you believe in that sort of thing.''

Chapter Five

Zac waited until the lights had been turned out in the ward, then he got up quietly, slipped on his clothes and left the hospital. The moon was just creeping over the treetops as he made his way along the unfamiliar streets.

From the many briefing sessions he'd had with Von Meter, Zac had a pretty good idea of the layout of the town. For weeks after that first night at the old man's town house, he'd pored over archived maps and documents, been drilled relentlessly by Von Meter and sometimes Vogel, until he knew the area around Oak Ridge as well as he knew his own Philadelphia neighborhood.

He also knew that getting inside the fence—getting to Kessler—would be no easy feat. The city was heavily fortified. Guards patrolled the borders and manned outposts around the clock, and no one was allowed inside the reservation without a pass or a purpose.

But Zac's more immediate concern was transportation. He had a lot to do tonight, and traveling on foot would soon eat up the precious few hours he had until midnight when the graveyard shift came on at the hospital. He didn't want to be reported missing when the nurses made their rounds. So far he'd been fortunate enough to escape the attention of the local authorities, but now that he'd come out of the coma, he knew they'd have questions.

And right behind the local authorities would come the Security and Intelligence Division and the FBI. If either agency became overly suspicious of him, they could arrest and detain him for weeks, months, possibly for the duration of the war. Zac couldn't allow that to happen. Keeping a low profile was imperative.

Hugging the buildings for cover, he made his way to the town square and from there, he headed north on Edgemont Avenue where Betty Wilson, the blond nurse, had mentioned that her aunt lived.

Eager for male companionship, the young nurse had freely imparted a wealth of information about her personal life. The seemingly endless chatter might have bored anyone else, but Zac had soaked it all in, knowing that the most mundane tidbit could prove useful in the future.

And he'd been right. Earlier, Betty had mentioned in passing that her aunt had taken the bus to Nashville to visit an ailing relative, which meant that her house would be empty, and, more important, her car would be unattended while she was gone.

The house was easy enough to find even in the dark, and, to Zac's relief, it did indeed appear deserted as he circled around to the back. Letting himself into the shed that sheltered the car, he whistled softly as his gaze lit on the 1937 Packard. The deep red fenders and upright chrome grill shimmered in the moonlight, but he took only a moment to appreciate the vehicle's sleek lines before he climbed inside, put the car in neutral and, with one foot on the ground and one shoulder against the frame, pushed until it began to roll silently down the drive.

The street in front of the house was on a gentle slope, and Zac kept the car coasting until he reached the end of the street. Jumping inside, he closed the door and prayed the battery wouldn't be dead as he pressed the starter button. To his relief, the engine caught and roared to life.

Heading south, he cranked down the window to let in the night air. There were no other cars on the road, and even over the steady purr of the V12 engine, the countryside seemed sleepy and silent. The farmhouses he passed along the way looked dark and desolate, the silhouettes eerie in the moonlight.

The whole night had a surreal quality to it, he decided. It felt a little like being trapped in a dream.

Two miles out of town, he turned onto a narrow gravel lane, drove for another quarter of a mile or so, then pulled to the side and parked. Farther down the road, he could see the lighted window of a house, which meant that people were still up. He didn't want the sound of the car engine to attract unwanted attention, and besides, from where he'd parked, it was only a short hike to the mine.

He got out of the car and glanced around, his senses on high alert. Crickets chirped in the ditches, and the occasional firefly flitted through the trees. But other than that, nothing disturbed the solace. It was a hot, still night, and a strange loneliness tugged at Zac's heart. Maybe he was just homesick, he thought wryly as he scanned the countryside. After all, he was a long way from Philadelphia. The Philadelphia he knew, anyway.

In the distance, a series of ridges rose, like humps on a camel, against the horizon. Zac knew the mine was up there somewhere. He searched his memory and began to walk.

As he neared the first house, voices drifted out of the darkness, and his first instinct was to melt into the nearby woods. Instead, compelled by curiosity, he followed the sound until he stood at the edge of the yard.

Three boys played chase in the moonlight, their childish laughter deepening Zac's strange melancholy. He knew he should keep moving, but he couldn't seem to make his feet obey. Finding a hiding place behind a hawthorn bush, he watched the boys dart in and out of shadows.

"You're it, Billy!" one of the older boys shouted.

"Am not!" the smallest boy retorted. "I tagged you!"

"You didn't even get close to me!"

"Did, too!"

The door to the house swung open and a stream of yellow light flooded into the yard. Zac automatically crouched lower in his hiding place.

"Boys!" a woman called. "Time to come in and get ready for bed."

"Ah, it's too early for bed!" one of the older boys complained.

"Yeah," the little one echoed. "It's too early for bed."

"No, it's not. It's after nine and you have to be

up early to get your chores done—'' The woman broke off as something shaggy shot past her legs.

The dog bolted from the doorway and made a beeline across the yard, straight for Zac, with all three boys in hot pursuit.

''Daisy, wait! Daisy!''

The dog, frantic with excitement, almost made it to Zac's hiding place before one of the boys grabbed her and drew her up short. The dog, straining to get loose, began to bark at the top of her lungs.

''What's the matter with Daisy?'' the smallest boy asked worriedly.

''There's something out there,'' one of the older boys said in a hushed tone.

''It's probably just a squirrel or something,'' the other one said with a shrug.

The woman hurried across the yard toward them. ''Daisy,'' she commanded. ''Stop that infernal noise! Heel, girl!''

To Zac's amazement, the dog fell whimpering to the ground, paws over her head.

The boys dropped to the ground around her. ''Good girl. Good Daisy.''

''You boys go inside like I told you,'' the woman scolded. As she neared the edge of the yard, Zac could see her more clearly. She was an older woman, tall and stoutly built with a harsh voice and nervous mannerisms. "I'll take care of Daisy."

The boys put up an argument, but the woman held her ground and finally the three took off across the yard toward the house. The woman bent down and patted Daisy's head. "What's out there, girl? What do you see?"

The dog continued to whimper. Straightening, the woman peered into the darkness. For a moment, it seemed to Zac that she stared straight at him, then her gaze moved on. "Is someone there?" she called. Then, more softly, "Have you come?"

When all remained silent, she turned back to the house. "Come, Daisy."

When the dog hesitated, the woman's voice rose harshly. "Come, Daisy! *Schnell!*"

THE FILMY CURTAINS FLOATED ghostlike on the breeze as Camille sank to the floor and folded her arms on the windowsill. Shivering, she gazed out over the lake. She still wasn't used to how quickly darkness fell over the remote countryside, how utter and profound the silence. It was hard to believe that half a world away, a war raged on.

But here, deep in the hills of Tennessee, she could hear nothing but the rustle of leaves in the sweet gums and more distant, the call of a whip-poorwill somewhere up on the ridge.

The plaintive cry brought on an unbearable loneliness, and grief constricted Camille's heart until she could hardly breathe. How much easier it would be just to go to sleep…and never wake up.

Would Adam be waiting for her on the other side?

The lure to find out was almost irresistible at times, but death was a luxury she couldn't afford. There was still too much to do. Too much was at stake.

But the pain… How much longer could she endure it? No matter how many months, years, decades passed, she knew it would never go away. She would always mourn her son. Ten years from now, she would still ache for his smile. Twenty years from now, she would still weep on his birthday. Time would not make any of that go away. Time would not ease her suffering.

Only one thing could do that.

She clutched the locket at her throat. On nights like this, when the pain was at its worst, Camille turned her mind to revenge.

In her heart of hearts, she knew it wasn't right to blame Zac for Adam's death. He was a victim of Von Meter's maniacal ambition just as the dozens, if not hundreds, of others who had passed through the underground bunkers at Montauk.

Subjected to radical experiments, Von Meter's "super soldiers" had been brainwashed and tortured, their lives and minds manipulated until little remained of the person they'd once been. Then they were cut loose to become drifters and mercenaries—or worse—who used their extraordinary skills for money, power and sometimes for a dark, twisted pleasure.

Devastated by the metamorphosis of the technology he'd pioneered, Dr. Nicholas Kessler—Camille's grandfather—had made it his life's work to seek out these men, to try and undo the damage done to their minds and to their lives.

Some of them could be saved. Some could not. Zac Riley was one of her grandfather's failures.

Although there had been a time when Camille thought that she, alone, could save him. The hubris of youth, she supposed. Or the blindness of love.

When she'd first gone to work in her grandfather's organization, he'd warned her that getting personally involved in the cases could prove disastrous. They could never be certain of their success, he'd reminded her, because some of the "triggers"—not unlike posthypnotic suggestions—had been planted so deeply in the victim's subconscious

that they remained hidden even under intense psy-
chotherapy.

But, in spite of her grandfather's warnings, Camille had been determined to save Zac...from Von
Meter and from himself. And, for a time, she'd suc-
ceeded. Or so she thought.

Then, one morning, she'd awakened to find him
gone. He'd left during the night without a word or
a note, the subconscious pull that compelled him
evidently a more powerful stimulus than his feelings for her.

That had been five years ago. Camille hadn't
seen him again until she'd found him half-dead in
the mine, and she knew his presence here could
mean only one thing. He was still under Von
Meter's control, and she would be a fool to trust
him.

ZAC HAD BEEN UNCONSCIOUS when Camille and the
boys had dragged him out of the mine and down
the side of the ridge, but he wasn't unfamiliar with
the terrain. Before he'd entered the wormhole, he
and Von Meter had flown down to Tennessee and
walked the area—or rather, he'd explored while the
old man had remained behind in their Knoxville
hotel—until he knew the area by heart.

To Zac's surprise, the countryside had hardly

changed. The road that led to the lake would be paved thirty years from now and a waterfront housing development would spring up during the boom of the eighties. But, for the most part, the region would remain rural and the trail up the face of the ridge would become even more overgrown with vines and brush until almost all traces of the early coal-mining days had disappeared.

Zac had spent hours studying local landmarks—the shape of the ridges, the contour of the lake—so that even sixty years back in time, he would still be able to get his bearings and pinpoint with some accuracy his location.

It had been time well spent because even in the darkness he had little trouble locating the trail and, a few minutes later, the mine. Clicking on the flashlight he'd taken from the nurses' station, he shined the beam around the tunnel until he once again had his bearings.

Following the railroad tracks that led back into the hillside, he made his way through the narrow confines until he came to a fork. Bearing right, he bypassed the first opening, moving deeper and deeper into the hillside until at last he reached a second tunnel. This time he turned left, and the passage eventually became so restricted that his shoulders brushed the sides as he crept along.

Deep inside the earth, his senses sharpened. Somewhere in the distance he could hear the drip of water and the occasional thud of loose gravel hitting the dirt floor. In spite of the nurses' conclusions, Zac didn't believe he'd been caught in a cave-in, but he was mindful of the danger just the same.

He still couldn't remember what had happened to him once he'd left the wormhole, but he had a strong suspicion that he'd been attacked in the mine and left for dead. He had no idea of the identity of his assailant or why someone wanted him dead. If the attacker knew who he was, that could mean only one of two things. Someone had followed him through the wormhole…or someone had been lying in wait for him. Either scenario presented a big problem. The presence of someone else from the future wasn't something Zac or Von Meter had counted on.

Ducking his head, Zac entered a small tunnel littered with rubble. Kneeling, he placed the flashlight on the floor beside him, then carefully began to dig through a pile of stones until he uncovered a weatherproof duffel. Quickly, he unzipped the bag and, shining the flashlight inside, rifled through the contents—a quarter of a million dollars in cash, sheets of ration coupons, counterfeit documents that would help him maneuver through governmental red tape and near the bottom, a .44 caliber Desert Eagle semiautomatic with a silencer. Everything was still there, including the gold medallion.

Picking up the weapon, Zac checked the clip, then returned it to the bag. Until he was released from the hospital, the gun and the cash were safer here than with him. Reburying the bag, he made sure nothing looked disturbed, then turned to retrace his footsteps through the mine.

As he neared the entrance, he heard voices somewhere outside on the ridge. Quickly, he doused his flashlight and ducked back into the tunnel just as someone stepped into the mine. Lantern light flooded the main cavern, but, from his position, Zac could see nothing.

He quickly contemplated his options. If he tried to make his way back into the mine, especially without benefit of his flashlight, he ran the risk of making a noise, no matter how slight, that would give away his presence. If he stayed where he was, he would surely be discovered should the newcomers decide to explore farther into the tunnel.

Hunkering against the wall, he waited. The voices had faded, but the light remained. Zac assumed they would be coming back, and, as he peered into the main shaft, a shadow appeared in the entrance. He had only a brief glimpse before he melted back against the wall. There were two of them, a man and a woman, by the sound of their voices. They spoke in low tones so that he caught very little of the conversation, but he could hear footsteps coming in and out of the mine and the occasional thud of what sounded like boxes or crates being stacked on top of one another.

Finally, there was a lull in the activity, and the man said in relief, "That's it. That's the last of it."

The woman's voice was muffled, as if she remained outside the mine. Zac couldn't make out her response.

"Don't worry. I'll come back later and move everything back into one of the tunnels," the man said. "We both need to get back before someone misses us." Shadows danced wildly against the walls as he picked up the lantern and swung around.

The woman said something and he gave a low laugh. "Yeah, too bad you didn't finish him off when you had the chance. But he'll get his soon enough. In the meantime, do whatever you have to do to keep those damn kids away from here."

The voices faded with the light, and, after a moment, Zac crept from his hiding place. Turning on his flashlight, he angled the beam against the far wall where the crates had been stacked. He walked over to examine them, but the lids were nailed shut and, without a crowbar or hammer, he couldn't get a look at the contents without damaging the containers. Next time, he'd come better prepared, he decided.

But even as the idea formed in his head, Von Meter's warning came back to him. *"...you must be extremely careful. You are being sent back to a very dangerous time. There will be those who would lure you into the intrigue of the day, but you must not get involved. There will be temptations, but you must resist them.* At any cost. *Even the smallest interference could be disastrous. Your mission is simple. You must prevent Dr. Kessler from tampering with those generators so that once the ship rematerializes, they can be shut off, thus triggering an event horizon. The wormhole will collapse, but everything else must remain the same. Is that understood?"*

Loud and clear, Zac thought. Whatever was in those crates was none of his business.

Leaving the mine, he drank in the fresh evening air as he made his way back down the ridge. As he emerged from the trees, moonlight glinted on the surface of the lake, and he paused for a moment to reconnoiter.

That was when he saw her.

She stood near the water's edge, her face pale in the moonlight. She wore a filmy dress that stirred gently in the breeze, and, as Zac watched her, she lifted her hand and drew it across her face, as if wiping away tears.

Why was she crying? he wondered. What was a woman like her doing alone in the moonlight weeping? Was she grieving someone she'd lost in the war? A lover? A husband?

He didn't want to think about that too closely, although he had no idea why. He didn't know her. Camille Somersby was a stranger to him and yet, from the moment he'd first laid eyes on her, Zac had sensed a connection. A strange bond he didn't understand.

Was it possible she could be the woman from his dreams?

He didn't see how. He was from another time, another place. How could he have known her?

"Are you the one?" he whispered into the darkness, and, although he knew she couldn't have heard him, she turned, as if sensing his presence.

He shrank back into the shadows, unwilling to confront her. His attraction to her was a dangerous thing, and he knew that if he was smart, he would keep his distance.

But there she was, crying in the moonlight....

"She's waiting for you. You have to go to her."

The voice was so clear in Zac's head that he whirled, almost expecting to find the boy standing behind him. But no one was there. Nothing stirred in the darkness but a soft breeze that ruffled the leaves overhead.

When he turned back around, the woman was gone, too.

Chapter Six

The blond nurse, Betty, could hardly contain her excitement the next morning when she came into the ward. She headed straight for Zac's bed. ''There's an FBI agent here asking questions about you,'' she said conspiratorially as she fluffed his pillow and straightened his cover. ''His name is Talbott. He's in with Dr. Cullen now.''

Zac tried to keep his voice neutral. ''What do you suppose he wants?''

''It's probably just a routine visit,'' Betty assured him, but she bit her lip in consternation. ''The government's pretty sensitive about security in this area. They're always snooping around, asking a lot of questions. It's a bit nerve-racking to have Uncle Sam constantly looking over your shoulder. But I guess they can't be too careful—'' She broke off. ''Here they come,'' she said under her breath.

Zac followed her gaze. Dr. Cullen and another man had just entered the ward, and, like Betty, they strode straight to Zac's bed.

"How are you feeling this morning, Mr. Riley?" Dr. Cullen asked briskly. His blue eyes were shadowed with fatigue and something that might have been disapproval as his gaze moved from Zac to the young nurse. But Zac had the distinct impression the doctor's annoyance had been aroused, not by Betty's presence, but by the man who stood beside him.

"This is Special Agent Talbott. He's with the FBI. He'd like to ask you a few questions if you feel up to it."

Zac shrugged. "Sure. How can I help you?"

The agent was tall and toughly built, with broad shoulders that strained against his black, ill-fitting suit. His hair was dark and he wore it slicked back, highlighting his pale skin and the patch he wore over his right eye. He gave Zac a cool appraisal before turning back to Dr. Cullen. "If you and your nurse would excuse us, I'd like to have a word with Mr. Riley in private."

Dr. Cullen's scowl deepened, as if the very sound of the man's voice grated on his last nerve. "Of course." He motioned Betty to follow him out, and she gave Zac one final pat before hurrying after the doctor.

Talbott glanced around the ward as if determining whether or not the other patients could overhear them. Not satisfied by what he saw, he came around the bed to stand at Zac's side. But, for the longest moment, he said nothing.

His silence didn't fool Zac. It was a waiting game. An intimidation ploy. He could see how it might be effective in certain circumstances. The man's size alone was imposing, and the way his Cyclops eye focused unblinkingly on his subject was more than a little disconcerting.

Zac stared back at him until Talbott finally glanced away. He paced to the end of the bed and back. "The doctor tells me you've made remarkable progress. You'll be leaving the hospital soon."

Zac shrugged. "I suppose so. But I'm a little surprised that my recovery interests the FBI."

The cold blue eye vectored in on him again. "Make no mistake, Mr. Riley. The Department of Justice, as well as the DOD, is very interested in your movements."

"Why?"

"This area is being flooded by strangers. Most of them are coming here for legitimate reasons, but there are some who are up to no good." His gaze deepened. "The battlefields may be overseas, but the enemy is here, within our borders. They are plotting our demise even as we speak."

"What does that have to do with me?" Zac asked, remembering the crates stacked in the mine.

"You may have the proper identification and papers, Mr. Riley, but I have a feeling there is more to you than meets the eye." Talbott's gaze narrowed. "Much more."

"I have nothing to hide," Zac said.

"For your sake, I hope that's true. Because the FBI has a saying—we always get our man." Glancing around, Talbott leaned in and said in a whisper, "I will be watching you. You can be sure of that...."

ON INDOCTRINATION, each Oak Ridge employee, civilian and military alike, was given a brochure with detailed instructions on the proper code of conduct while behind the fence. The government's motto was What You See Here, What You Hear Here, Let It Stay Here. And to reiterate that point, signs posted throughout the compound cautioned workers and residents to be on the lookout for enemy agents.

But, in spite of all the precautions taken by the government, including around-the-clock patrols, checkpoints and screenings, breaches in security were inevitable. On any given day, as many as twenty thousand people passed through the gates into and out of the reservation. It was not hard to imagine that a spy, or even a saboteur, could somehow slip through the cracks.

Although constantly aware of the threat, Camille tried not to let herself get caught up in the espionage paranoia. She hadn't traveled sixty years back in time to root out spies or to interfere with the progress of the war. She was here for one reason only: to keep Dr. Kessler—her grandfather—safe from Von Meter's dastardly plan, whatever it might be.

At the thought of her grandfather, she couldn't help but smile forlornly. The first time she'd caught a glimpse of him in Oak Ridge had been a surreal moment to say the least. The man she'd left behind in California was in his nineties and growing feebler by the day. The Dr. Kessler of 1943 was only a few years older than Camille, probably no more than thirty-five. He was a stoop-shouldered, studious-looking man with dark hair and eyes radiating such warmth and kindness, Camille's heart had ached with the knowledge that the grandfather she knew, the Nicholas Kessler of the future, was not long for his world.

She despaired of the time when she would lose him, too. Her father had been killed in the last days of the Vietnam War, and her mother had died ten years later. Her grandfather had been her only family until Zac had come into her life. And then Adam. Now they were both gone. Adam was dead, and Zac... Zac was still alive, but he was as lost to her as her son.

Forcing herself from the painful reverie, Camille tried to concentrate on her work. She was one of dozens of young women employed in the administrative offices on the reservation whose duties included filing the thousands of top secret documents associated with the Manhattan project.

From her desk, she could literally watch history being made. The men who passed through the offices, laboratories and the plants themselves wore color-coded badges which denoted their security level and bore names that would someday be famous in scientific circles: Ernest O. Lawrence, J. Robert Oppenheimer and Arthur Holly Compton.

"You look as if you're a million miles away."

Camille started slightly, then glanced up with a smile. A young woman with nondescript features held out a coffee cup. "I thought you could use a break."

"Thanks," Camille said, accepting the cup.

Alice Nichols perched on the corner of Camille's desk and took a tentative sip of her own coffee. Blond and blue-eyed, she was several years younger than Camille, probably not yet twenty-five with an easygoing personality and an infectious smile. She'd once confided to Camille that she'd led a very sheltered life until the outbreak of the war. Then, over her father's objections, she'd left school to join the WACs, hoping to be sent overseas, but instead had found herself buried in paperwork at Oak Ridge.

She glanced around, then leaned toward Camille. "Have you noticed all the VIPs coming in and out of here today? Something big is in the works."

Camille shrugged. "I haven't noticed anything out of the ordinary. What's going on?"

Alice glanced around again, then lowered her voice to a conspiratorial whisper. "I hear Kessler is making waves again."

Camille kept her tone neutral. "Really? What's he done?"

The young woman hesitated as if struck by a sudden bout of conscience. "I really shouldn't say anything…."

But, of course, she was dying to. She'd let it slip once that she had a male friend who worked in Dr. Kessler's lab and who, despite rules to the contrary, made frequent nocturnal visits to the all-female dormitory on the reservation where Alice lived.

The arrangement wasn't unusual. In fact, the number of out-of-wedlock pregnancies inside the reservation was a growing concern for the government.

"Something's going to happen on the fifteenth," Alice confided. "And Kessler's trying to stop it. It's all very hush-hush. My friend was afraid to talk about it, even with me. He says it has something to do with a U.S. Navy ship, and that if all goes well, the war could be over in a matter of weeks, if not days."

The Philadelphia Experiment, Camille thought, her heart starting to pound. The fifteenth was less than a week away. Whatever Zac was up to, he would make his move before then, and she would have to be prepared to stop him.

"What's the matter?" Alice asked in alarm. "You look a little pale all of a sudden."

Camille tried to smile. "Nothing. We should probably get back to work."

"Oh…sure." Alice got up and headed back to her desk. But, once she was seated, Camille glanced up and saw that the young woman was gazing at her speculatively. Did she suspect something? Camille wondered. Her paperwork was all in order, her cover solid. And yet she'd had a nagging feeling for days that someone was watching her.

Was that someone Alice Nichols?

WHEN ZAC OPENED HIS EYES, Camille stood at his bedside. For a moment, he thought that he might still be dreaming, but then she smiled, and the desire that stabbed through him was all too real.

If anything, she was more beautiful than he remembered. Her hair was swept back from her face in the style of the day, and she wore only a hint of lipstick. Zac remembered reading somewhere that lipstick had been exempted from the government's wartime restrictions on the manufacture of luxuries because they'd determined that the cosmetic was too important to maintaining gender lines and morale. *Good call,* he thought, gazing at Camille's lush mouth.

''How are you today?'' she inquired in a voice that might have come straight from his dreams. It was soft and feminine, but with an edge of determination that made Zac wonder again about her motives. Who was she, and what was her interest in him?

He wanted to be flattered by her attention, but, unlike the nurses who seemed to be starved for male attention, Camille Somersby appeared to be a woman on a mission.

What that mission was and how it involved him, Zac had no idea. But he intended to find out.

"I'm being released today," he informed her.

"Yes, I know. I spoke to Dr. Cullen." Her tone was matter-of-fact, but Zac thought he detected a hint of nerves in the way she clutched her purse in both hands. "That's why I'm here...to extend my offer once again."

"For a room, you mean."

"Yes. Have you changed your mind?"

He studied her features. "Not really. I guess I'm still wondering why someone like you would make such an offer to a total stranger. You don't know anything about me. About my character. I could be a criminal, a murderer for all you know."

Something flickered in her eyes. "I'm not afraid of you, Mr. Riley."

"I can see that." He paused. "Maybe I'm afraid of you."

She looked startled. "What do you mean?"

"There's something about you...." He trailed off and shook his head. "Every time I see you, I get the impression we've met before. But I can't place you."

She hesitated, then lifted her shoulders. "Maybe

a part of your subconscious was aware of me in the mine. Maybe that's what you remember.''

"Maybe," Zac said doubtfully. "At any rate, I'm not exactly in any position to look a gift horse in the mouth.''

"Meaning you accept my offer?''

His gaze met hers. "Meaning, under the circumstances, I would be a fool not to.''

SHE WASN'T USED TO the Studebaker, Zac thought as he watched her struggle with the gears before pulling onto the street. She released the clutch smoothly enough, but something about the way she groped for the gearshift on the steering column made him think that perhaps she hadn't been driving all that long.

He supposed that wouldn't be unusual for the time. A lot of women still considered driving a male pursuit, although the war was rapidly changing old perceptions. Since the start, women had gone to work in record numbers, and their contributions at home and abroad would be a vital part of the effort.

Camille Somersby appeared to be one of the new breed of independent women. Her navy suit was trim, tailored, all business. She wore matching shoes, but her legs were bare, Zac noticed, because nylons, like so many other things, were hard to come by in wartime.

He glanced up to find her gazing back at him. She'd caught him staring at her legs, but rather than appearing offended, she gave him a slight smile and returned her gaze to the road.

A new breed of woman, indeed, he thought.

A few minutes later, she pulled off the main road onto the gravel lane that led back to the lake. As they neared the water, they passed a white clapboard house with three boys playing in the yard. The same boys Zac had seen the night before. When they saw Camille's car, they raced toward the road, waving and calling out her name.

She stopped and rolled down her window as they bounded up to the vehicle. "Davy, Donny, Billy, I'd like you to meet Mr. Riley. He's the man you helped rescue from the mine the other day."

The boys' eyes widened as they took him in. The two older ones looked to be around twelve, Zac decided, with features similar enough to be twins. The younger boy, Billy, was probably no more than five, a freckle-faced carrot-top with a disarming grin.

"Hey, mister, what the heck were you doing in that mine anyway?" Davy asked bluntly.

"That's none of your business," his brother, Donny, informed him.

"Sure it is. We saved his life, didn't we?"

"Yeah," Billy agreed. "We saved his life." He beamed at Zac, obviously pleased with himself.

"What do you mean, *we?*" Davy demanded. "You weren't even there."

"I was, too!" Billy defended. "I went and got Miss Camille just like you told me to."

"I was just trying to get rid of you so you wouldn't be in the way," Davy said. He turned to Zac. "It was Miss Camille and me who pulled you out of that mine. You'd have been a goner for sure if it wasn't for us."

"Sounds like I'm indebted to all of you," Zac said diplomatically.

"Me, too?" Billy asked eagerly.

"Of course, you, too." Camille reached out and tousled his hair. "Your job was very important that night, Billy. You did just as you were told. I'm very proud of you. I'm proud of all of you," she added. "But I meant what I said. I want you boys to stay away from that mine. You hear me? That place is dangerous."

"In the meantime, whatever you have to do, you keep those damn kids away from here."

Zac frowned as he studied Camille's profile. Was

it possible she'd been in the mine last night? He thought back over what he'd seen and heard. The man had done most of the talking, but Zac was certain his companion had been female. She'd spoken so softly he hadn't been able to hear her responses. Camille had a soft voice. And when he'd emerged from the trail last night, she'd been standing beside the lake. Had she arrived mere minutes before he had?

That would explain why she seemed so eager to provide him a place to stay. If she thought he might have stumbled upon her nefarious activities, then it stood to reason she'd want to keep a close eye on him.

His gaze flickered over her again. She was gorgeous, mysterious and, if his instincts were to be trusted, dangerous. The thought crossed his mind that Camille Somersby just might be Oak Ridge's version of Mata Hari.

"Do I have your promises that you'll never go up there again?" Camille demanded of the boys.

"Yes, ma'am," Billy readily agreed.

"Yes, ma'am," Donny echoed.

Davy said nothing. That kid was trouble, Zac thought, his gaze meeting the boy's.

Davy's gaze was direct, knowing and more than a little defiant.

Zac's frown deepened. Between the kid and Camille, he looked to have his hands full.

"THIS IS IT." Camille pushed back the curtain revealing a tiny, converted porch with windows on one side overlooking the lake and on the other, the woods that sprawled up the face of the ridge. The bare plank flooring creaked ominously as Zac stepped into the room and glanced around. The space was sparsely furnished with a narrow bed and an old beat-up dresser shoved against a whitewashed wall. But the view from the windows more than made up for the lack of luxuries.

"This is great," he said. "I'm sure I'll be very comfortable out here."

"You might not say that come morning," Camille warned. "It's like an oven in here when the sun comes up."

"I'm sure I'll manage." Zac placed his meager belongings on the bed and walked over to the windows to stare out at the lake. Before he'd left the hospital, Betty had put together a care package for him, complete with several changes of clothing she'd borrowed from her cousin and some toiletries she'd used her own ration coupons to purchase at the store in town.

Zac intended to pay her back, but he had to be

careful. He didn't want to arouse suspicions by being too generous with his counterfeit ration coupons, nor did he want to raise Betty's hopes that there could ever be anything other than friendship between them. She was a nice girl, attractive and bright, but he wasn't there to get involved with the locals. He wasn't there to get involved with anyone, he reminded himself as he turned to Camille.

She smiled.

"There will be temptations, but you must resist them. At any cost."

He turned quickly back to the lake. Behind him, she said, "I suppose I should do something about dinner. Are you hungry?"

He was, in fact. "What can I do to help?"

"Nothing. You should probably lie down and rest for a while. I'll call you when it's ready."

He turned back to her. "But I have to earn my keep, remember?"

"Oh, you will," she promised. "And then some."

CAMILLE WAS GLAD that Zac wasn't around to see her struggle with the meal preparations. She still wasn't used to the oven, which was gas and had to be lit with a match, or the lack of modern conveniences such as mixers and blenders and food processors. There was a refrigerator, however, with old-fashioned rounded corners, and the stove itself was really quite beautiful with its curved legs and hand-painted porcelain.

Like everyone else, Camille relied heavily on canned goods, including meat, but tonight she'd splurged on a chicken which she intended to roast and serve with new potatoes and homemade biscuits.

Shedding her jacket, she rolled up her sleeves, kicked off her shoes and set to work. While the chicken and potatoes roasted in the oven, she measured out flour, baking powder, milk and Crisco—packaged in glass rather than tin—then kneaded the mixture until she had the desired consistency. Next she rolled out the dough and, using the top of a fruit jar, cut out the biscuits. She greased the pan and placed the bread in the oven to bake.

The thermostat on the oven didn't seem to work so she had to hover nearby, checking constantly to make sure nothing burned. By the time the meal was finished, she was covered in flour and her face was flushed from the heat. Placing the biscuits in a basket and the chicken and vegetables on a platter, she left everything on top of the stove to stay warm while she went to freshen up.

Pinning up her hair, she splashed cold water on

her hot face and neck, then changed out of her skirt and blouse into a thin cotton dress.

Emerging from the bathroom, she walked back into the kitchen and glanced toward the porch. She hadn't heard a peep out of Zac since she'd left him earlier. If he was napping, she hated to wake him, but the food would soon be cold if she didn't.

Hesitating for only a moment, she went over and put her ear to the curtain, listening for signs of life. When she heard nothing, she called softly, "Zac? Dinner's ready."

When there was still no answer, she drew back the curtain and peered inside. He was lying on the bed, presumably asleep, but he looked so still that, for a moment, Camille's heart stopped. Then she saw the rise and fall of his chest, and she drew a breath of her own.

Crossing the room to the bed, she gently shook his shoulder. "Zac? Are you okay?"

His eyes flew open, and before Camille knew what was happening, he'd grabbed her arms and pulled her down on him. Then he reversed their positions until he was lying over her, his knee pressed into her abdomen, his hand around her throat.

Chapter Seven

He released her almost instantly and Camille scrambled away from him, clutching her throat as she got to her feet. "What do you think you're doing?"

He looked horrified as he stood. "I'm…sorry. I didn't mean to hurt you. It was just a reflex."

"A reflex?"

"I was asleep." He ran a hand through his hair. "You startled me awake. I didn't mean to hurt you," he said again.

He looked so contrite and puzzled by his own actions that Camille's anger faded. She'd seen a similar reaction in him before, and had learned early in their relationship not to come up behind him or awaken him abruptly. His reflexes were almost superhuman, and, once upon a time, she'd too easily cast aside the reality of just how dangerous he could be. But she remembered it now.

She was suddenly aware of a lot of things about Zac Riley. The past that lay between them. The fact that he was shirtless.

His muscles gleamed in the late-afternoon light, and, in spite of herself, Camille's gaze slipped over him.

She remembered how he'd looked gazing down at her, his body moving against hers. In those long, dark nights they'd spent together, he'd taken her closer to paradise than any man ever had, and those memories had kept Camille awake on more nights that she cared to remember.

Her gaze lifted, and something sparked in Zac's eyes. An acknowledgment of the attraction that was as keen and deadly as summer lightning.

Slowly, he reached for his shirt. "Sorry," he muttered. "It was a little warm in here earlier."

It was even warmer now, his eyes told her. Camille tore her gaze from his. "You don't have to apologize. This is your room. You can do what you want in here. Within reason," she felt compelled to add.

He grinned. "You mean no female guests after midnight?"

Camille wasn't amused. The thought of Zac and another woman was an image that had haunted her for years. But he didn't know that, of course.

"I came to tell you that dinner is ready," she said stiffly.

"I'll be right there." He slipped on his shirt. "Just give me a minute to freshen up."

"Sure." At the curtain, Camille glanced over her shoulder. Zac was buttoning his shirt, and he paused, his gaze lifting to hers. For a moment, it seemed to Camille that time stood still, then the world began to turn again, and she hurried through the curtain.

ZAC WALKED INTO the tiny kitchen to find Camille chipping away at a block of ice in the sink. "I've made lemonade," she said. "Though I'm afraid it'll be a little on the tart side, what with the sugar shortage and all. But at least it'll be cold. That is, if I can get enough ice chipped off here."

"Here, let me have a go at it." Zac walked over to the sink. To his surprise, she relinquished the ice pick without argument. She even turned her back to check on the food. That took some courage after what had just happened between them in the bedroom.

Or maybe she knew she wasn't the one in danger, Zac thought, his earlier doubts coming back to him.

He dismissed them.

Easy enough to do with the way she looked this

evening. The heat only enhanced her natural beauty. Earlier, in her prim and proper suit, she'd seemed remote and unattainable, but now with her hair pinned up and her skin shimmering, she looked sexy as hell.

When she caught him staring at her, she turned quickly back to the stove, obviously flustered by something she saw in his eyes. "I...thought we could eat on the front porch." She brushed back her hair with the back of her hand. "It'll be a little cooler out there."

"Sounds good," Zac agreed. He helped her carry everything out and only when they were seated, watching the sun set over the lake, did she seem to relax.

"This has to be one of the most beautiful spots on earth," she said softly.

"And to think, some people don't even know this place exists."

She glanced at him. "How about you? Have you ever been in this part of the country before...Mr. Riley?"

"You called me Zac earlier."

"I thought you were asleep," she accused.

"I was, but I thought I heard my name just before I woke up. At any rate, please call me Zac. It seems only right, now that we're living together."

She frowned. "You're leasing a room from me. I think the distinction is important. At least to my reputation."

"Of course," he agreed easily. "But you have to admit, these are strange times. A week ago, we didn't even know each other, and now here we are…." He trailed off on a shrug. Lifting his glass, he reached over and clinked it against hers. "To victory," he said.

Was it his imagination, or did she hesitate before she lifted her glass and returned the salute. "To victory," she murmured.

They ate in silence for a few minutes, then she said nonchalantly, "You never answered my question. Have you been here before?"

"Once, a long time ago."

"You have…ties here?"

What was she after? he wondered. He glanced up. "I told you in the hospital, I came here looking for a job."

"Behind the fence."

"Yes."

"What kind of work do you do?" Her gaze met his then flickered away, as if she was afraid she might give herself away.

"I've done a little bit of everything including construction, but I'm open to new possibilities." He took a sip of the tart lemonade. "Did you mean what you said about speaking to someone on my behalf?"

When she hesitated, he quickly said, "Of course, you've already done enough. Giving me a place to stay is more than I could have hoped for."

Something dark flickered in her eyes, something that drew a shiver up Zac's backbone. "I didn't do it out of the goodness of my soul. I expect to be repaid."

Yes, and that's what worries me.

What, exactly, did she want from him?

AFTER THE DISHES WERE DONE and the leftovers put away, they took a stroll down by the lake. By this time, only a pale shimmer remained of the sunset and dusk fell gently over the countryside. With the twilight came a breeze off the water and a melancholy that tugged at Camille's heart.

She missed her grandfather although he was only a few miles away. She missed Zac although he stood right beside her. She missed Adam although he would always be in her heart.

He seemed especially close tonight, maybe because she could see him in Zac. She could see, in Zac's face, what Adam might have looked like as a man.

She turned, blinking back tears.

"What's wrong?" Zac asked in concern.

She wiped a hand across her face. "It's…personal."

"Did you lose someone in the war?" When she didn't answer, Zac said, "I don't mean to pry. It's just…you seem so sad."

She tried to shrug away the sorrow. "We live in sad times."

"Was he a lover?" There was a strange urgency in Zac's voice.

Camille turned in confusion. "What?"

"The person you lost. Was he a lover? Your husband?"

She shook her head. "My son."

She heard him draw a sharp breath. "My God," he whispered. "I had no idea. I'm sorry. How long—"

"A year ago," she said. "I really don't want to talk about it."

"I understand." But she could hear the questions in his voice. How did it happen? How old was he? What was his name?

She remembered that day in the hospital when he'd first come to and asked about someone named Adam. She'd wondered then and she wondered now how he'd known. How could he possibly have known?

Adam hadn't been born until after Zac left. She'd had no contact with him until she'd seen him in that mine nearly a week ago. How could he have known about her son? About *their* son?

"What about your husband?" Zac asked.

She didn't bother to correct him. "He's gone, too," Camille said almost angrily.

Something in her tone must have warned him against further inquiry. He turned to stare at the lake, and a deep silence fell between them.

Presently Camille became aware of the sound of laughter in the distance, following by splashing.

"Sounds like the boys are taking a swim," Zac mused.

"I hope Mrs. Fowler is keeping an eye on them," Camille said worriedly.

"Who's Mrs. Fowler?"

"She's their housekeeper. Mr. Clutter hired her to watch after the boys while he's at work, but from what I can tell, the boys are pretty much left to their own devices."

"I guess that's lucky for me," Zac said.

Camille glanced at him. "What do you mean?"

"If she kept them on a tight leash, I might have died in that mine."

"That's true." Camille sighed. "But I still worry

about them.'' It was the mother in her, she supposed. Adam had died before she'd fulfilled all of her maternal instincts.

She listened to the childish laughter, the sound bittersweet in the darkness. Then her heart froze as the shrieks of laughter turned to screams.

She clutched Zac's arm. ''Something's wrong.''

He took off running with Camille close on his heels. As they neared the shore, she could see two distant figures in the dark water. At the edge of the lake, Donny struggled to launch the dinghy the boys used for fishing.

''Donny, what's wrong?'' Camille called.

He looked up, his expression frantic. ''It's Billy. He followed Davy out into the deep water and he can't swim.''

In a flash, Zac tore off his shirt, kicked off his shoes and dove into the water. Camille was right behind him, but Zac soon outdistanced her. She could see him closing in on the boys as Davy valiantly tried to keep his brother's head above water. But he would tire soon. If Zac didn't reach them in time, both boys could drown—

Billy's head slipped underneath the water, then Davy's. After a moment, Davy resurfaced, but there was no sign of Billy.

"Hang on," Camille whispered. No sooner had the plea left her lips than she saw Zac reach Davy. He said something to the boy, then dove. A few seconds later, Camille dove, too.

It was so dark beneath the surface that she feared they would never be able to find the child, but then she saw Zac a few feet away, and he had Billy.

They both surfaced, gasping for breath. Zac struck out for the bank with the child in tow, and Davy and Camille followed. When they reached shallow water, Zac picked Billy up and carried him to the beach. He positioned the unconscious child on his back and turned his face to the side. A trickle of water oozed out of Billy's mouth.

Working quickly, Zac knelt with one leg on either side of Billy's hips, then placed his hands, one on top of the other, on Billy's upper abdomen. Using the heel of his hand, he performed a series of quick upward thrusts as water flowed from Billy's mouth. After only a few seconds, the child began to cough. Then he began to cry.

Camille knelt and put her arms around him, cradling him to her. "It's okay, sweetie. You're going to be fine." But the more she soothed him, the louder he howled.

A door slammed nearby, and then, after a moment, Mrs. Fowler came hurrying out of the twilight toward the water. "What's wrong? I heard someone yelling."

"Billy almost drowned," Camille said bluntly. "The boys shouldn't be swimming alone. Especially not after dark."

"But I only left them for a moment," the older woman defended. "And I thought Donny and Davy would keep an eye on him."

"It's not their responsibility to keep an eye on him," Camille said accusingly.

"Take it easy," Zac murmured.

He was right. The harsher her tone, the more upset Billy became.

"We should get him inside and into some dry clothes before shock sets in," Zac advised. He bent and took the boy from Camille. Billy had been tense, almost hysterical in her arms, but he relaxed completely against Zac. His tiny arms wound around Zac's neck as he placed his head on Zac's wide chest.

The sight brought a gasp from Camille. And then the sting of tears. Seeing Zac like that...with Billy in his arms...

She had never seen him hold Adam. It was a loss she'd always felt keenly, but, for the first time, she put her bitterness and pain aside long enough to acknowledge what Zac had lost through no fault of his own.

He carried the boy into the house and, at Billy's insistence, helped him into his pajamas and then into bed.

Donny and Davy hovered nearby, hero worship shining on their faces, while Mrs. Fowler lurked in the doorway, wringing her hands.

"Is there a telephone?" Zac asked over his shoulder.

"Yes. The government put in a new line when they built the reservation."

"Call the operator and have her connect to the hospital. See if you can get a doctor out here."

"But he seems fine now," Mrs. Fowler protested.

Zac whirled. "Either you make the call or I will, but the boy needs medical attention. Is that understood?"

"I know how to use the phone," Davy said. "I'll call Dr. Macy."

"He joined the army," Donny reminded him.

"Have the operator get hold of Dr. Collins," Zac said. "Tell him it's an emergency."

Davy ran off to the phone while Mrs. Fowler lingered in the doorway. Outside, a car door slammed, then, moments later, footsteps sounded down the hallway. Daniel Clutter appeared in the doorway, his eyes wild with concern. When he saw Billy, he rushed over to the bed.

"Billy, son, are you all right? What happened?"

Zac stepped back from the bed to make room for the worried father. "He's going to be fine, but I think it would be a good idea to have a doctor look him over just to be on the safe side."

"Yes, of course." Daniel sat down on the edge of the bed and placed his hands on Billy's shoulders. "What happened, son?"

"He went in the deep water and almost drowned," Donny said. "But Mr. Riley saved him. You should have seen him, Pop. He swims like a fish."

"Faster," Davy said as he came back into the room. "And then he pressed on Billy's stomach and water shot out of his mouth."

Camille happened to be watching Mrs. Fowler as Davy described the procedure, and the older woman's face went still with shock. Then her gaze narrowed on Zac.

Zac placed his hand on Davy's shoulder. "Did you get the doctor?"

"He said he'd come right away."

"Good." He glanced at Camille. "We should

probably clear out of here so that Billy can get some rest. He's had quite a night.''

''You saved his life,'' Davy said solemnly.

''Well, it was only fair since you saved mine.''

Daniel Clutter stood up and stuck out his hand to Zac. ''I don't know how I can ever thank you.'' He was a plain-looking man with a careworn face and a receding hairline.

''No thanks necessary. I'm just glad the boy is going to be okay.''

Guilt flickered across Daniel's face as he gazed down at Billy. It was the bane of all single parents, Camille thought, that you could never be in two places at once.

Outside, Zac and Camille retrieved their shoes from the beach, then walked silently home. As they entered the house, Camille turned on a lamp. ''We should probably get out of these wet clothes, too.'' Then, as if concerned by how that might have sounded, she glanced up. ''I mean, we don't want to catch cold…or anything.''

''Not to mention ruining your floor.''

''I'm not worried about the floor.'' She drew a long breath. ''The boys were right, Zac. You were amazing. If it hadn't been for you—''

''You would have rescued him yourself.''

"But I'm not as strong a swimmer as you. We all three might have drowned."

"Then it's lucky I was there," he said softly.

Camille nodded, the emotions of the night tightening her throat. "I have to be up early in the morning so I think I'll turn in."

"Good night, Camille."

"Good night."

She hurried inside her bedroom, closed the door and turned the lock.

As if that would keep temptation at bay, she thought.

Undressing, she quickly dried off, then drew on her nightgown. As she sat down at the bureau to brush out her wet hair, a knock sounded on her bedroom door.

Her heart thudded against her chest. She hesitated for a moment, then got up and went to answer it. Zac stood on the other side, still in his wet clothing.

Camille stared up at him. "Yes?"

"I have to ask you something." His gaze on her was dark and intense. Almost accusing, she thought nervously.

"What is it?"

"Why didn't you ask me how I did it?"

Her heart thudded again. She knew what he

meant, but she pretended she didn't. "I don't know what you're talking about."

"Why didn't you ask, Camille?" Her name on his lips drew a shiver up her spine. "Aren't you curious about the procedure I used?"

"The only thing I care about is that Billy is still alive. You saved him." Her gaze met his, and now it was she who sounded slightly accusing. "I only wish you could have saved *my* son."

Chapter Eight

The next morning, a man Camille had never seen before approached her desk at work. She knew that he was someone with a high-level security clearance or he would never have been allowed in offices that housed so many top secret documents.

"Miss Somersby?"

"Yes." As Camille stared up at him, a cold chill shot through her. He was one of the most formidable-looking men she'd ever seen—tall and ruggedly built, with dark hair swept back from a pale face and an eye patch that gave him not so much a rakish appearance, but more the look of a satyr.

His gaze was cold and unblinking as he stared down at her. "I'm Special Agent Talbott, FBI." He showed her his credentials. "I wonder if I might have a word with you."

"Of course," Camille said reluctantly.

Talbott scanned the room where dozens of sec-
retaries and file clerks busily went about their jobs.
Camille glanced around, too, and her gaze met Alice Nichols's. The young woman looked up from
her typewriter and lifted a querying eyebrow. Camille shook her head slightly and turned back to
Talbott.

"Is there someplace we could speak in private?"
It was more of a command than a request. Camille
nodded and rose. She led Talbott across the hall to
a small break room furnished with a few wooden
tables and chairs. He motioned to the table farthest
from the door and they both sat.

"What's this about?" Camille asked bluntly.

The blue gaze regarded her for a moment before
he said, very softly, "You have a man living in
your home. A Mr. Zac Riley. I want you to tell me
everything you know about him."

Camille frowned. "Why? Has he done something
wrong?"

"I'll ask the questions, if you don't mind. What
can you tell me about Riley? Where is he from?
Why did he come here?"

Camille shrugged. "I assume he came here for
the same reason we all did. To find work."

"What was he doing in that mine?"

"I don't know. The nurses at the hospital seem

to think that he went inside to get out of that terrible storm that came through here last week.''

''What does *he* say?''

Camille shrugged again. ''He doesn't seem to remember many of the details before or after the accident.''

''How convenient,'' Talbott muttered. His gaze lifted. ''I'm surprised that you seem to know so little about him.''

''Why? He's my tenant. We aren't friends.''

''And yet you invited him into your home. My mother would tell you that you are playing with fire, Miss Somersby.''

''He needed a place to stay and I had a room for rent. It's as simple as that. Surely you're aware of the housing shortage around here. A lot of people have invited strangers into their homes. Some might say it's the patriotic thing to do.''

''Are you a patriot, Miss Somersby?''

Something about the question—or perhaps it was his tone—set off warning bells in her head. ''Of course I am.''

''You would do your patriotic duty, then, to insure an Allied victory?''

Camille frowned. He was making her more nervous by the moment, but she tried not to show it. ''What are you getting at?''

He leaned toward her, and she had to fight the urge to shrink away from him. "What if I were to tell you that we know of an enemy spy in Oak Ridge, living and working among us? We know this agent has recruited at least one person to his cause, and together they are plotting something big, even as we speak."

"Why don't you arrest him then?" Camille said.

"We don't yet know his—or her—identity. But if they're not found, and soon, the damage to *our* cause could be catastrophic."

Camille shook her head. "I don't understand. What is it you think I can do? I'm just a file clerk."

"You are a file clerk with a high-level security clearance," he reminded her. "I'm asking you to keep your eyes and ears open. Be on the lookout for any suspicious activity at work…and at home."

Her gaze went cold. "You want me to spy on Zac Riley for you? Is that what you're asking?"

"You're in a unique position to keep an eye on him for us. If he does or says anything the least bit dubious, I want you to report back to me. But I must advise extreme caution." His gaze deepened. "I have a feeling your Mr. Riley is a very dangerous man."

You have no idea, Camille thought with a shiver.

NORMALLY, CAMILLE and Alice Nichols timed their lunch breaks so that they could eat together in the cafeteria, but a fresh batch of files kept Camille late and by the time she was able to tear herself away, the young woman was nowhere to be found. Camille wondered if she'd snuck away for an assignation with her lover.

Making her way along the wooden walkway, Camille tried in vain to stay out of the mud, but it oozed between the slats so insidiously there was no getting away from it. People were so accustomed to the muck by now that they fondly likened the reservation to the Klondike gold-rush days. And as with most frontier-type settings, the population of the town was noticeably youthful. There was one big difference, however, that Camille had noted. The pervasive presence of the military was unique to the government town site.

As Camille walked along, she thought about her conversation with Talbott and his assertion that an enemy spy had infiltrated Oak Ridge and that he or she—along with at least one recruit—was planning something big.

Could their scheme have something to do with her grandfather's work? she wondered. The Philadelphia Experiment was scheduled for August 15, less than a week away. Was it possible that enemy agents had gotten wind of the project and were planning to somehow sabotage the ship? Or worse, to steal secret documents that would allow them to recreate the experiment?

A part of Camille wanted more than anything to destroy the experiment herself. How many lives could be saved—including her son's—if the technology that had led to Project Phoenix had never been developed? If Von Meter's megalomania had never been given free rein?

But Camille's grandfather had cautioned her against such interference. She wasn't there to tamper with history or play God. She was there to insure that Von Meter and his minions didn't, either.

Entering the cafeteria, she quickly filled a tray, then found a table in a quiet corner where she had a view of the door. Alice Nichols came in a few minutes later, and before Camille could wave her over, the young woman headed toward the other side of the room. She sat down at a table occupied by a man who had his back to Camille. As she watched, Alice leaned across the table and smiled. There was something intimate in that smile, Camille thought. Something seductive about her body language as she gazed intently into his eyes.

Then she pulled back, and as she placed her handbag on the table, a paper fluttered to the floor.

She and her companion reached for it at the same time, but the man's arm was longer. He plucked the paper from the floor, but rather than return it to Alice, he casually stuffed it into his pocket.

It was all done very quickly, very casually, so as not to call attention to the action. Camille glanced around the cafeteria. She was almost certain no one else had even noticed the exchange, and she was left wondering what she should do about it.

Nothing, of course. She couldn't interfere, and besides, it might have been nothing more sinister than a love note.

A moment later, the man got up and strode to the door. As Camille watched him, the hair at the back of her neck bristled. There was something about him...

He turned at the door to glance over his shoulder, and she had a quick glance of his profile. The pale skin, the dark hair, the eye patch...

Talbott. Camille drew a sharp breath as recognition shot through her. She'd seen him before. Not just this morning in her office, but in a different time, a different place...

A vision came to her suddenly. She and Adam playing baseball in the park. A man standing in the shadows watching them. Then he stepped into the light, and, when he removed his dark glasses, there was something odd about his eyes...something that chilled Camille to the bone.

She felt that same chill now as she watched Special Agent Talbott disappear through the door.

ZAC WAS PLAYING CATCH in the front yard with Billy when Camille got home from work late that afternoon. She sat in the car for a moment and watched them. It was like having a glimpse at what might have been, she thought with a pang. And a reminder of what she had lost.

Billy came running up to her as soon as she got out of the car. "Guess what? Zac is teaching me how to play baseball!"

"That's wonderful," Camille managed to say over the lump in her throat. "It's about dinnertime, though. Don't you think you'd better be heading home?"

He turned to Zac. "Just a few more minutes. Please? Pretty please?"

The lump in Camille's throat threatened to cut off her breath as Zac ruffled Billy's hair. "Miss Camille's right. You need to run along home now." When the boy started to protest, Zac said, "Go on, now. We'll play again tomorrow."

"You promise?"

"I promise. And you remember what you promised me."

"If I stay away from the mine, you'll teach me how to throw a curveball?"

"That's right. Now run along and see if you can keep out of trouble."

Billy beamed up at Zac, then took off for home.

Zac turned to Camille. "Is something wrong?"

She glanced away. "No, why do you ask?"

"You seem upset."

"It's been a long day—"

"It's more than that. I saw your face when you first came up. What is it, Camille?"

Something in his voice, in the way he said her name, brought tears to her eyes. "It's just...my son loved baseball," she heard herself saying. "We were playing catch in the park the day he died."

"God," she heard Zac mutter as she turned and hurried inside the house.

A moment later, he followed her in. "I'm sorry. I had no idea."

She stood at the window, staring out at the lake. "How could you?"

"What happened?" he asked softly.

"He ran out into the street after a ball and was struck by a car."

Camille squeezed her eyes closed as images

bombarded her. The screams, the sirens, the pounding of her own heartbeat. The terrible knowledge as she'd cradled her son in her arms that he was already gone....

She turned and started toward her bedroom. "I'll get changed and then start dinner."

"No, don't go. Tell me about him."

There was a strange plea in Zac's voice, one that tore at Camille's heart. "I...can't. I can't talk about him. Not with you. Not with anyone." She turned back to the door, but Zac caught her arm.

"Camille—"

His gaze on her was dark and mysterious and...gentle somehow. It wasn't pity she saw in his eyes, it was compassion. It was confusion. It was all the emotions Camille felt, too.

He reached up and thumbed a tear from her face. She shivered at his touch. At the memories the caress evoked.

For the longest moment, they stood that way, gazing into one another's eyes, his hand cupping her face. And then, very slowly, he dipped his head toward hers.

Camille jerked away. "I have to get changed." Before he could protest, she fled into her room, closed the door, then leaned back weakly as she tried to slow her racing heart.

For a moment out there, she'd been certain that Zac meant to kiss.

And, for a moment, she was pretty sure she would have let him.

A STRANGE NOISE AWAKENED Camille. She lay in the darkness, trying to pinpoint the sound. She thought at first it was some night creature up on the ridge, but then she realized it was closer than that. It was coming from somewhere inside the house.

Her heart pounding, she got up and slipped silently across the room. Opening the door, she peered out. Nothing seemed amiss. Nothing stirred in the darkness. Then she heard the sound again, and she realized it was coming from the back porch. Zac was in trouble.

Camille didn't bother to knock. She drew aside the curtain, catching her breath at what she saw.

Zac lay naked on top of the covers. He shivered so violently the bed actually shook beneath his weight, and he gasped for breath, as if he couldn't draw enough air into his lungs.

Camille hurried across the room to the bed. She knew the danger of awakening him suddenly, but she couldn't allow him to suffer like that. Tentatively, she bent and shook his shoulder. The moment he opened his eyes, she jumped back.

But instead of the violent reaction she'd expected, he lay stone still, his gaze seeking hers in the darkness. "Camille?"

She smoothed nervous hands down the sides of her cotton nightgown. "You were having a nightmare."

"It's…freezing…in here." His teeth chattered as he spoke.

The temperature was stifling, in fact, but Camille reached out and handed him the quilt that had slipped to the floor. Zac drew it around him, still trembling. "Where am I?" he finally said.

"You don't remember?"

He glanced around. "I—" Comprehension dawned on his face, and he fell back against the pillow. "Oak Ridge…1943," he whispered.

"That's right."

He licked his lips. "I'm thirsty. Do you suppose…I could have a glass of water?"

"Of course."

Camille was relieved to have something to do. She hurried from the room and took her time filling a glass from the tap. When she came back, Zac had put on his pants, and now he sat on the edge of the bed, his face in his hands. He looked up expectantly when she came in.

"Here's your water."

"Thanks." He took the glass and drained the contents like a man dying of thirst.

"Would you like some more?" Camille asked.

He set the glass aside. "No, that's fine. Look, I'm sorry I woke you up."

"No problem. I'm sorry I woke *you* up. But…I was worried about you. You seemed so distressed."

He glanced away. "It's a recurring nightmare."

"Do you want to talk about it? It might help."

He ran a hand through his hair. "Nothing helps. Except…"

"Except what?"

"A distraction."

Camille's heart started to pound. What was he suggesting?

Who was she kidding? She knew *exactly* what he was suggesting.

When he stood, she inadvertently took a step back. "I should go," she murmured, "Let you get back to sleep."

"I won't be able to sleep. I never can after the nightmare." He started slowly toward her.

Camille back stepped again. "Well…then I should get to sleep. I have to get up early—"

"Don't go," he said softly. He put out a hand, but he didn't touch her. Instead, he braced himself against the wall, as if still not quite steady on his feet. "I need to ask you something."

"What is it?" Camille's heart pounded so hard she could hardly breathe. Why was she having this kind of reaction to him? It wasn't as if anything was going to happen between them. Was it?

"Why do I feel I know you?" he asked almost desperately.

She twisted the locket at her throat. "I told you. On a subconscious level, you probably remember me from the mine."

"That doesn't explain why your name feels so familiar on my lips." He reached up and trailed his hand down her throat, then pressed a fingertip to her pulse. Camille knew that it was racing. Now he knew it, too. "Why do I know your taste, your touch…the way your body moves when we make love…."

Camille gasped. She would have protested, but she was rendered speechless by his words, by his nearness, by the memory of his body, naked and hard against hers.

His fingers encircled her neck and he pulled her to him. "I know you, Camille. I know what you like," he whispered, and then he kissed her, proving to them both just how right he was.

He did know her. Still. After all this time.

He kissed her so deeply Camille's legs began to tremble. She wound her arms around his neck, threaded her fingers through his hair and kissed him back. Kissed him deeply. Kissed him the way *he* liked to be kissed.

Because she knew him, too. Still. After all this time.

He drew back in shock. "My God—"

She pulled him to her, capturing his lips, tasting him with her tongue. Groaning, he drew her nightgown over her head and tossed it aside. Then he picked her up and carried her to the bed. Camille didn't resist. Instead, she lay back and let him gaze at her.

"I want you." His voice trembled with emotion. With need.

"I know."

His hand skimmed her breast, and Camille closed her eyes, capturing his hand between hers and holding it to her heart. "I want you, too. It's been so long…."

"Who are you?" he whispered harshly.

Camille opened her eyes. He still stared down at her, but the desire had faded, replaced by a cold, black suspicion. She shuddered at that look and reached for her nightgown.

Zac caught her wrist. "Answer me, damn it. Who are you?"

Camille tried to shake off his hold. "Let me go."

His grasp tightened on her wrist. "Not until I get some answers."

"Answers to what?" Camille asked angrily. "I don't know what you're talking about."

"What the hell do you want from me?"

"Nothing! I offered you a place to stay because you had nowhere else to go."

"I don't believe you. I don't believe you're who you say you are."

And Camille didn't believe how cold his eyes had grown, how savage his voice sounded. In the blink of an eye, he'd changed into a man she didn't know, but had always feared.

"Why did you come in here tonight? What did you hope to gain by seducing me?"

"*Seducing you?*" Her voice quivered with outrage.

"Don't try to convince me you were swept away by passion. That's not the action of a woman still grieving for her husband, much less a dead son."

Her heart twisted. "How dare you?" she whispered. "How dare you use Adam to try and hurt me that way—"

Zac went deathly still. "What?"

His hold on her relaxed, and Camille scrambled away from him. She got up, grabbed her nightgown and, clutching it to her, backed toward the door.

"What did you say?" Slowly he got to his feet.

"Stay away from me," Camille warned.

"You called him Adam." He sat back down on the bed as if all his strength had suddenly drained away. When he looked up again, Camille had never seen such anguish on anyone's face.

Her anger faded, and she took an inadvertent step toward him.

"Get out of here," he said in a voice she didn't recognize. "Get the hell out before I do something we both might regret."

Chapter Nine

Camille wasn't all that pleased to see Alice approach her desk the next day. Since she'd seen the young woman with Talbott in the cafeteria, her suspicions were aroused. What exactly was Alice's relationship with Talbott, and what had happened to the young research assistant she'd been seeing? According to Alice, he worked in a highly classified area of the Y-12 Plant. Had he been passing her top secret information? Information that she, in turn, had been relaying to Talbott?

Alice held up a metal spool and smiled ruefully. "I just broke my last typewriter ribbon," she said. "I guess it's been reinked one too many times. Need anything from the supply closet?"

"No, thanks." Camille kept sorting through her files, but the moment Alice left the room, she got up and followed her out.

The clatter of typewriters followed her down the long, narrow hallway. Alice was just ahead of her, and, when the girl turned to glance over her shoulder, Camille darted into an empty office. Peering around the corner, she watched as Alice unlocked the supply-room door and disappeared inside.

Within moments, the door opened again, and Talbott stepped into the hallway. He glanced around, then strode off in the opposite direction from where Camille stood. A moment later, Alice emerged looking very much like the cat that ate the canary as she headed back toward her office.

THAT AFTERNOON, a summons came from Dr. Kessler's office. Camille couldn't have been more surprised. She'd only seen her grandfather in passing. They had yet to formally meet, but every time Camille saw him, she was tempted to tell him who she really was. She held back for two reasons. One, learning her true identity could be detrimental to both their futures, and two, he would probably think her insane and have her thrown off the reservation.

So Camille held her tongue, but when she entered his office that afternoon, she was struck again by how different he was from the man she knew as her grandfather. Different…and yet so many things about him were endearingly familiar. The stooped shoulders. The gentle eyes. And like his twenty-first-century persona, he cared little for his appearance. Today his suit was rumpled, his bow tie all askew and his shirt was badly frayed at the collar and cuffs.

He glanced up when she walked in, and once again his eyes took her aback.

"Miss Somersby, isn't it?" When she nodded, he motioned her to a chair across from his desk.

Camille sat and opened her steno pad.

"You won't need that," he said. "I didn't call you in here to take dictation."

Camille waited curiously for him to continue.

"I've been watching you ever since you came on board here," he said. "And I've been impressed by what I've seen."

"Thanks," Camille murmured, but she couldn't help wondering why he'd called her in.

"I've seen you eating alone in the cafeteria from time to time. I take it you don't have many friends here?"

She shrugged. "I haven't been here all that long."

"No, but I can tell you're a serious young woman. You aren't prone to idle chatter like so many of the others. You're hardworking, efficient and, more important, discreet. That's why I feel I can ask a favor of you.''

Camille stared at him in surprise. ''What kind of favor?''

''Do you know how to type?''

''Yes.''

''In that case…'' He pulled a folder from his desk and held it out to her. When she would have accepted, he hesitated. ''First, I have to be certain that the contents of this folder will stay between the two of us. I'm not exaggerating when I say your prudence could be a matter of life and death.''

Camille nodded. ''I understand.''

''Inside this folder, you will find a series of handwritten letters,'' he explained. ''I want you to type them for me, but it is imperative no one else know of their existence.''

Again Camille nodded.

''Do not make any carbon copies,'' he warned. ''Once you've finished, bring both sets of letters back to me along with the ribbon from your typewriter. Understood?''

''Yes, of course.'' Camille took the folder and stood.

When she got to the door, her grandfather said anxiously, ''One more thing, Miss Somersby.''

She turned back. ''Yes?''

He seemed at a momentary loss for words. "Is there any possibility that you and I have met before?"

Camille almost smiled. "I don't think so. Why?"

"There's a familiarity about you. I noticed it the first time I saw you, but I couldn't quite put my finger on why it was so."

"Maybe I remind you of someone," Camille suggested.

He looked thoughtful. "Yes, I think that must be it," he mused. "It's your smile, I think. It reminds me of a young woman I knew back in New York. A colleague at the university where I taught before the war. I've often wondered what happened to her...." He trailed off, as if no longer addressing Camille.

Elsa Chambers, she thought. The woman who would become her grandmother.

"Perhaps when the war is over you should look her up," Camille suggested.

"Oh, I don't know." His voice grew slightly gruff. "I'm sure she's married by now. She was a very beautiful woman. At any rate, I hardly think she'd remember me."

"You might be surprised," Camille murmured.

But she didn't think he heard her. Nicholas Kessler appeared lost in thought.

WHEN CAMILLE FINISHED the letters, she slipped them into the folder, along with the cotton ribbon from her typewriter, and carried them down the hall to her grandfather's office. She knocked, then stepped inside, stopping abruptly when she realized he wasn't alone.

"You've finished the reports, I see." He put a slight emphasis on the word *report*.

"Uh, yes." Camille walked over and handed him the folder. Before he could take it from her, however, Talbott reached out and intercepted the package.

"You didn't tell me that you work directly for Dr. Kessler," he said.

"You didn't ask," Camille countered.

"Is there a problem?" her grandfather asked in confusion. "Miss Somersby has been cleared for top secret access. She and the girls in the pool deal with thousands of classified documents on a daily basis. Why are you concerned about the work she does for me?"

"I'm concerned with every aspect of security in this city." Talbott stared down at the folder for a moment, then handed it to Kessler. "Your *reports*." He, too, put an emphasis on the word.

"Thank you." Her grandfather took the folder and placed it on his desk, then calmly clasped his hands on top of it. "That will be all Miss Somersby. Unless Special Agent Talbott has anything further."

"No, nothing," he said with a slight smile. "I think Miss Somersby and I understand one another perfectly well."

ZAC USED THE FLASHLIGHT he'd found in Camille's kitchen to search the mine. The crates that he'd seen two nights ago were gone from the main cavern, but he had a feeling they were still hidden somewhere inside the mine.

About a hundred yards into the tunnel, he found them and quickly set to work. Placing the flashlight carefully on the ground, he used a crowbar to pry loose the lid on one of the crates, then whistled when he saw the contents. Nestled in a bed of sawdust was enough dynamite to blow up the whole damn ridge.

The other crates contained weapons, documents and even more explosives.

Returning the lids to the crates, Zac quickly hammered them back in place, then glancing around to make sure he'd left nothing behind, he hurried even farther into the mine to retrieve his own weapon.

A little while later, he surfaced from the trees at the bottom of the ridge and quickly scanned his surroundings. It was the middle of the day and no one appeared to be about, but he knew he couldn't be too careful. Whoever was stockpiling that dynamite would more than likely keep a close eye on the mine.

He returned the hammer and crowbar to the toolshed behind the cottage, then, hurrying inside the house, he shoved the satchel containing the money and his gun beneath the bed on the porch. Camille didn't particularly strike him as the kind of person who would snoop in his personal belongings, but, then again, there was something about her he still didn't quite trust.

Not wanting to dwell on Camille—or the kiss they'd shared the evening before—Zac went outside and sat down on the front porch to think about what he'd just seen. Dynamite. Weapons. Fake documents. By all indications, he'd stumbled upon the lair of a professional saboteur, but because he couldn't tamper with history, there wasn't a damn thing he could do about it.

CAMILLE WAITED with dozens of reservation workers outside the gate for the bus that would take them home that evening. Some of the employees had as much as a two-hour commute, but Camille would get off just outside Ashton, where she would have a short walk to the cottage.

It would be nearly dark by the time she got there, but it couldn't be helped. She'd driven to work for the past several days, and now her ration coupons were running low, forcing her, like so many others, to ride the bus.

She didn't really mind. The bus ride and then the walk would give her time to prepare for seeing Zac again. She'd purposely left for work earlier than usual that morning, not only because she had to catch the bus, but because she'd desperately wanted to avoid another confrontation with him.

She frowned as she spotted the bus's headlights in the distance. The kiss last night had caught her completely off guard even though she'd wanted it to happen since the moment Zac had opened his eyes in the mine. She'd dreamed about that kiss for years, yearned to have his arms around her, holding her close, whispering to her that the world was right because they were together.

But the world wasn't right. They were at war, and Camille had a mission to complete. A mission that could very well force her to choose between the man she loved…and the future.

But that choice had already been made. She'd made it the day she'd convinced her grandfather that she was the right person for the job, that she, and she alone, could stop Zac Riley.

"But you still have feelings for this man," her grandfather had said kindly. "Don't underestimate the power of that love, my dear."

"I'm not," Camille denied. "But I know what's at stake. I know what has to be done. And if I still have feelings for Zac, then I have to believe that somewhere deep in his subconscious he still feels something for me, too. I can use those feelings. I can make him trust me...."

The bus pulled to a noisy stop outside the barricade, drawing Camille's attention back to the present. As she boarded the bus, she noticed Alice Nichols just ahead of her in the crowd, but she made no move to get the young woman's attention. Instead Camille pretended she didn't see her and took a seat a few rows back from where Alice sat.

Twenty minutes later, when the bus stopped in Ashton, Alice got off. Camille hesitated for a moment, then followed her, even though the next stop would have been much closer to the cottage. Now she would have a two-and-a-half-mile walk in the deepening twilight.

The young woman hurried away from the bus stop, but Camille lingered for a moment to mingle with the crowd. When she felt it was safe, she followed Alice, keeping enough distance between them to remain undetected.

A few blocks over, Alice stopped to admire something in a store window. A moment later, a car pulled to the curb beside her. Casting a furtive glance up and down the street, Alice rushed over and climbed inside.

The vehicle pulled away from the curb and headed in Camille's direction. Backing quickly into a doorway, she tried to disappear into the shadows as she watched the car go by her.

The window was down, but she caught only a glimpse of the man behind the wheel. It was enough. She recognized him immediately.

The driver was Daniel Clutter.

BETTY AND VIV gushed over the lemonade Zac served them, despite the liquid's tartness. He had made it for dinner that night, a peace offering to Camille, but he hadn't known what else to do when the nurses had shown up unexpectedly at the cottage. They'd walked all the way from town and looked so hot and dusty and...expectant somehow standing on the front porch that Zac had felt compelled to offer them a cool drink. It was the least he could do after all they'd done for him.

And if he were honest with himself, he had to

admit that he wasn't exactly immune to their charms. They were both attractive young women, amusing and flirtatious, and their competitiveness with one another sometimes prompted outrageous behavior. They were both talkers, too, veritable founts of information about the townspeople and many of the strangers who'd arrived in the area to work behind the fence.

"We stopped by your neighbor's house to pay our respects, but, unfortunately, he wasn't home," Betty said, accepting a fresh glass of lemonade. She took a long sip.

"You mean Daniel Clutter?" Zac asked in surprise. "You know him? He's not a local, is he?"

"He only moved here a few months ago, but he's a widower so naturally Betty already knows him," Vivian said dryly.

Betty wrinkled her nose at her friend. "You didn't exactly object when I made the suggestion to stop by and see him."

"No, but I should have. Did you see the way that awful woman looked at us? Why, you would have thought we were a couple of cheap floozies." Viv folded her hands primly in her lap. "I didn't appreciate her implications."

"She wasn't the most hospitable person I've ever

met," Betty agreed. She turned to Zac. "Have you met her?"

"Mrs. Fowler? Yes, I've had that privilege."

Betty giggled at his sardonic tone. "She has the strangest colored eyes. Have you noticed? They're so dark, almost black, and very cold. Not at all like yours." She peered at Zac through the falling twilight. "You have dark eyes, too, but they're very warm and...passionate."

"Oh, brother," Viv muttered.

"What?" Betty asked innocently. "You know very well that I'm partial to brown eyes."

"Oh, really? Then how come you were going on and on about Dr. Cullen's eyes just this morning? 'They're the most gorgeous shade of blue,'" Vivian mimicked. She brought her clasped hands up to her cheek. "'When he looks at me, I swear, I could just lose myself in those eyes.'"

Betty bristled at the imitation. "You're just jealous because you don't have a boyfriend."

"And you do?"

"I...might."

"Who is he?" Viv demanded.

"You don't know him."

"I don't know him?" her friend asked in disbelief. "I know everyone you know."

Betty smiled. "That's what you think."

"Then who is he? What's his name? And why have I never seen you with him?"

"A woman never divulges all her secrets." Betty's smile turned cagey. "Isn't that right, Zac?" She batted her lashes so fast and so furiously that Zac worried she might take flight.

Before he could respond, a voice said from the twilight, "I didn't know we were having a party tonight. I would have tried to get home earlier."

At the sound of Camille's voice, guilt shot through Zac although he had no idea why. His visit with Viv and Betty was innocent enough, and, besides, he and Camille were hardly more than strangers.

But the guilt persisted, and he got awkwardly to his feet. "The girls just came out to see how I'm getting along."

"Did they?"

At her frigid tone, the nurses rose hastily, as well. "My goodness, where did the time go? We really should be getting back to town."

"Yes, we have to go," Viv agreed. "Thank you so much for the lemonade. It's nice to see that you're doing so well after such a painful ordeal."

"It's almost dark," Zac said. "Maybe I should walk you back to town."

"Nonsense. We'll be fine—" Viv's words were cut off on a grunt when Betty nudged her in the ribs.

"Well, if you insist…" Betty said.

Vivian turned to glare at her friend. "It's five miles into town and back. Mr. Riley is still recuperating."

"Of course. What was I thinking?" Betty murmured. "It's just that you look so…healthy." Her gaze admired him until Viv grabbed her arm and pulled her toward the road.

"I still don't feel right about this," Zac called after them. "Are you sure you don't want me to walk you at least part of the way?"

Before the blonde could answer, Viv said, "Betty's uncle lives just down the road. We promised we'd drop by and see him on our way back. He'll give us a ride into town."

After their voices had faded in the distance, Camille brushed past Zac and went inside the house. He waited for a minute, then followed her.

She didn't look up when he walked in, but continued to fiddle with the radio.

"I found some tools in the shed out back," he informed her. "I'll get to work on the roof first thing in the morning."

She remained silent.

"Are you upset about something?" he finally asked.

She glanced up, her blue eyes glittering with anger. "Why would I be upset?"

"I don't know. But it's obvious something has you all hot and bothered. If you're mad because the girls dropped by—"

She snapped off the radio so violently the knob came loose in her hand. She threw it against the couch. "If you want to entertain your girlfriends while I'm at work, that's your business. But I would just as soon you find someplace else to do it."

Zac stared at her in disbelief. "They're not my girlfriends. They're nurses who happened to take very good care of me while I was in the hospital."

"Yes, I saw the way they took care of you." Camille gave him a scornful glance. "If they give every patient the same treatment, I'm surprised anyone ever leaves the hospital."

"Are you jealous?" Zac asked incredulously. Hopefully.

Her eyes widened in outrage. "*Jealous? Jealous?* Why on earth would I be jealous? I couldn't care less whom you spend time with."

"Really?" Zac cocked his head as he continued to study her. "Because you could sure fool me with this attitude of yours."

"Did it ever occur to you that I might want to come home from a long day at work to some peace and quiet?"

"Maybe you should have thought about that before you invited me to stay here. Which brings me back to something I've been wondering about for days. Why did you invite me here?"

"We've been through this before," she said wearily. "You needed a place to stay and I had a spare room for rent. I thought it would be a beneficial arrangement for both of us."

"Even though I don't have a job? No visible means of support? But there's always that leaky roof, right?"

"The roof, the porch." She shrugged. "A dozen things need attention around here, but if the arrangement isn't working for you, then by all means, find yourself other accommodations. Stay, go. Do what you want. I'm going to bed."

She started out of the room, but Zac quickly crossed the floor and caught her arm. She whirled to glare up at him. "Let go of me."

He did so immediately, but there was still a connection between them. A bond that Zac didn't understand, but he was pretty sure she did.

"About last night—"

"I don't want to talk about it," she said angrily.

"Well, I do. What happened between us doesn't happen between strangers. It felt right. It felt… familiar."

"I'm not surprised." Her eyes blazed up at him. "You obviously have a penchant for female company."

"That's not what it was, and you know it. There's something between us, Camille. Why won't you be honest about it? Is it because…you still have feelings for your son's father?"

She stared at him in shock, and for a moment her face crumpled, as if she was about to lose control of her emotions. Then she stiffened her spine and hardened her resolve. When she looked up at him again, her mask was firmly back in place. "Leave me alone, Zac. Just…leave me alone."

Chapter Ten

Camille's eyes flew open at the sound of a creaking floor. Someone was walking through the house. A moment later, she heard the back door open and close softly as someone exited.

Rising quietly, she slipped across the room to the window and stared out. She saw nothing at first, but then she spotted Zac hurrying from the house, and a moment later, he disappeared into the trees on the ridge.

Camille quickly dressed, then slipped her gun into her bag, grabbed a flashlight from her dresser and raced out of the house.

Picking her way along the trail, she paused now and then to listen to the darkness. When she arrived at the clearing, Zac was nowhere to be seen. She assumed he'd entered the mine, but she had no idea what he was up to.

She stepped through the opening and paused just inside to listen once again. All was silent at first, but then from somewhere deep in the tunnel, she heard what might have been footsteps.

Following the sound, she angled her flashlight beam at the floor hoping to avoid detection. About a hundred yards or so in, she saw light emanating from one of the other tunnels and she quickly doused her own light.

Creeping toward the opening, she pressed herself against the wall, waited a heartbeat, then peered around. A lantern hung from a peg on the wall, and a bedroll had been flung in one corner, along with several tins of food.

Wooden crates were stacked against one wall, and tools had been scattered about on the floor.

But still no Zac.

Was this his hideout? Camille wondered. Had he brought all this stuff in here?

She ducked her head and stepped into the small roomlike tunnel. Walking over to the crates, she checked to see if she could open one, but the lids were nailed shut.

Glancing around for something to pry open the tops, she spotted a crowbar among the tools on the floor, grabbed it, and then set to work on the nearest crate.

She was so busy at the task that she failed to see the shadow on the wall looming over her until it was too late.

Slowly she lifted her head as the hair on the back of her neck prickled in warning. Everything went still inside her. But even as fear shot through her veins, her hand tightened around the crowbar as she readied herself for battle.

Before she could even turn, a strong hand grabbed her wrist. Another hand clamped over her mouth, and a voice whispered in her ear, "Don't move. Don't even breathe."

STRUGGLING FIERCELY to free herself, Camille bit his hand, and Zac stifled a curse. "What are you trying to do, get us both killed?" he said against her ear. "They're coming back. We've have to get out of here."

He dragged her to the entrance, and when she put up no resistance, he thought it safe to release her. The moment he freed her, she spun to face him, her eyes blazing in the lantern light, but when he put a finger to his lips, she nodded.

She followed him into the main tunnel, and he took her hand, guiding her along the narrow passageway until they came to another opening. He pulled her inside, and only then did Camille speak.

"What's going on? What's in those crates—"

She broke off at the sound of distant voices. As they drew nearer, she clutched Zac's arm.

They stood in total darkness. He couldn't see her expression, but he could hear her rapid breathing. When she pressed against him to lift her mouth to his ear, her breasts grazed his chest, and the only sound Zac heard then was the pounding of his own heart.

"Who are they?" she whispered.

He shook his head. When she didn't move away, Zac put his arm around her, pulling her even closer. She didn't resist. Not for a moment. It was probably her fear that made her so willing, but Zac wanted to believe it was something else.

Resting his head against the wall, he tried to get a grip on his emotions. This was crazy, he told himself. Totally insane. They were both in danger here. The world was at risk and all he could think about was how she felt in his arms. How much he wanted to kiss her.

The voices grew louder, then faded as the interlopers stepped into the tunnel containing the crates. All was silent for a moment, then the woman's laughter echoed through the darkness. The laughter soon turned into murmurs and then groans of ecstasy.

CAMILLE SQUEEZED HER EYES closed in embarrassment. She wasn't a prude, but eavesdropping on someone else's lovemaking was hardly an activity she enjoyed.

On the other hand...

The feel of Zac's body against hers was something that held great appeal. He was in perfect shape. Lean and muscular. A man in his prime.

And Camille was a woman who hadn't had *any* man in a very long time. Not since Zac had left in the middle of the night five years ago.

Don't think about that now, she warned herself.

But...she had to think about it. She had to remember how easily he'd left when Von Meter had summoned him. It wasn't his fault. Camille knew that. He hadn't left of his own accord, but the result had been the same. He'd abandoned her, and now she couldn't trust him. She would be a fool to trust him.

Presently the moans subsided, and after a few moments, the two lovers left the mine.

Camille tried to pull away, but Zac held her against him. His lips brushed her hair, and only then did he release her.

THEY DIDN'T SPEAK UNTIL they were home, safely inside the cottage. Camille placed her bag on the kitchen table and turned expectantly. "What was all that up there? Who were those people?"

"I'd hoped to find that out tonight," Zac said, running a hand through his hair. "Then you came along and my plans had to change."

"Are you saying you knew they were going to be there?"

He shrugged. "If not tonight, another night. I knew they'd come back sooner or later for the contents in those crates."

"What's in those crates?"

He hesitated. "Enough explosives to take out this whole ridge."

Camille's eyes widened. "Saboteurs?"

"I'd say that's a distinct possibility," Zac said grimly.

"Then we have to stop them. We have to—" Camille broke off as her grandfather's warning came back to her. *"You mustn't interfere with history, Camille. No matter how tempted. No matter how justified your actions seem. You are there for no other reason than to contain Von Meter's madness."*

She walked over and glanced out the window, a chill going up her spine. "We're constantly warned at work to be on the lookout for signs of espionage, but a terrorist act—"

"A what?"

Too late, Camille realized her mistake. Terrorism had been around for centuries, but the term had not come into wide use until well after World War II.

"Sabotage," she corrected.

He looked at her strangely. "Why do I get the feeling there's something you aren't telling me about all this?"

"There's not. I don't know any more than you do."

His gaze narrowed. "I think you do know. I think you know a hell of a lot more than I do. I think there's a reason you used the term *terrorist* so casually. It's the same reason you didn't question my use of the Heimlich maneuver on Billy and the same reason you invited me into your home. And do you know what else I think?" He moved slowly toward her.

Camille trembled at the look in his eyes.

"I think you are a very dangerous woman."

CAMILLE TOOK A LONG BATH before bed that night, hoping the hot water would help her relax and help her avoid Zac.

He was asking too many questions, putting two and two together, and she didn't know what to do about it. How to head him off. She'd gotten careless, slipped up, and now the whole mission could be in jeopardy.

Maybe she should just come clean with him, Camille thought as she finally climbed out of the tub and toweled off. Appeal to that part of him not under Von Meter's control. The part of him that might still harbor feelings for her.

But those feelings hadn't been strong enough before, and Camille saw no reason to believe the situation would turn out any different now. She couldn't trust him. She didn't dare trust him. It was as simple as that.

She pulled her nightgown over her head, then opened the door and glanced out. The house was dark and quiet, and she assumed Zac had already turned in. Slipping into her bedroom, Camille closed the door and got into bed, hoping that a good night's sleep might help her see things more clearly in the morning.

But she'd no sooner drifted off than a loud banging on her bedroom door startled her awake. Her eyes flew open and she bolted upright in bed.

"Camille? Open the door. I want to talk to you."

Camille didn't want to talk to him. That was the last thing she wanted. She drew the covers up around her. "Can it wait until morning?"

"No. Open the door."

When she still hesitated, Zac said angrily, "Open the damn door, Camille, or I swear I'll break it down."

Getting out of bed, she pulled on her robe as she hurried across the room. She only meant to open the door a crack, but Zac was having none of that. He put his hand against the wood and pushed, forcing Camille to step back. Then he flung the door open and stood on the threshold, glaring down at her.

"Who are you?"

"You…know who I am."

"I don't know a damn thing about you, and yet…" His expression made Camille shiver. "I *know* you."

"I told you before. You remember me from the mine—"

"Is that so?" His icy gaze swept over her. "Then how do you explain this?" Her gold locket gleamed in the moonlight as he held it up.

Camille's hand flew to her throat. She'd taken off the necklace before her bath, then forgotten to put it back on. Zac had found it, opened it and now he knew. Everything.

"If we're nothing but strangers, why do you wear a picture of me in your locket?" he demanded.

Camille had no ready explanation. She stared at
him helplessly.

He opened the locket and gazed down at the pictures inside. "The boy...he's your son?"

She nodded.

"Why do I know *him?*"

"You don't," Camille said.

But he didn't seem to hear her. He studied the
tiny photograph, his expression a mixture of anger,
confusion and wonder. "Why do I know his face,
his voice?"

Camille put a trembling hand to her mouth.

"I know him, Camille. I've seen him. I've even
dreamed about him."

She gasped. "That's not possible." And yet he'd
awakened from his coma asking about Adam.

Zac lifted his gaze. "Why do you keep a picture
of your son next to mine? Answer me, damn you."

Camille drew a long breath. "Because he was
your son."

Chapter Eleven

He couldn't have looked more stunned if she'd slapped him. He turned toward the door, and Camille thought that he meant to leave, but then he whirled, grabbed her arms and backed her up against the wall.

Camille didn't cower from him. She stood her ground and stared him in the eye. "It's true. You were Adam's father."

His grasp tightened. "It can't be true. You're lying."

"I'm not lying, Zac."

His gaze burned into hers. "You have to be. *Because it's not possible.* I've never been here before. Do you understand?"

She drew another breath. "Yes. But you said it yourself earlier. There's a reason why I didn't have questions about how you saved Billy, or why I used the term terrorist so easily."

Realization sparked in his eyes, and then his expression hardened. "You came through the wormhole?"

"Yes."

His fingers dug into her flesh. "Who sent you? Von Meter?"

"No. Nicholas Kessler."

"Kessler?"

"He's my grandfather," Camille said. "I came here to protect him."

"From who?"

"From…you."

He stared at her in disbelief. "You think I came here to harm Kessler? I didn't. That's not the mission's objective."

"And now I don't believe *you*," Camille said.

He released her and backed away. Then he spun toward the door and strode out of the room without another word. Camille waited a few seconds before following him. When she entered the living room, he was standing by the window, bathed in moonlight. She caught her breath at the look on his face. It was hard, angry, resolved. And yet vulnerable somehow. Infinitely vulnerable.

As she watched him, his gaze dropped to the locket he still clutched in his hand. For the longest moment he said nothing, and when his gaze finally lifted to hers, his expression was shuttered.

"Tell me about him."

"I'll try," Camille said softly. "But it's still hard for me to talk about him."

"You said he was struck by a car."

Her throat tightened. "Yes. He died in my arms at the scene."

Zac put a hand to his face and squeezed his eyes closed. "Was I there?"

"No. You didn't even know about Adam. At least…that's what I've always believed. But now I think you must have seen him at some point. How else would you have known his name, his face? They must have arranged it somehow."

"They?"

"Von Meter. Project Phoenix."

He closed his fist over the locket. "What do they have to do with Adam?"

"Everything. He was your son."

The implication seemed to strike at his very core. Pain flashed across his face as he turned back to the window.

Camille walked over and sat down on the edge of the couch. "How much do you remember about Project Phoenix?"

He shrugged. "It's based on technology developed during the war. This war. It's being developed even as we speak. A U.S. warship will disappear from Philadelphia Harbor on August 15. According to Von Meter, the ship will enter some kind of parallel dimension and travel forward in time. When it returns, a wormhole will open connecting the past to the future. I know it sounds crazy, but..." He turned. "Here we are."

"Yes," Camille murmured. "Here we are." His gaze was so intense that she had to glance away. She clasped her hands in her lap and studied them for a moment. "What else did Von Meter tell you?"

"The same technology that will make that ship disappear will become the basis for Project Phoenix. After the experiment, your grandfather will lobby successfully to have government funding cut off. The project will be forced underground, and, without oversight, the research will eventually expand into controversial areas—interdimensional phasing, psychotronics, thought control and telekinesis."

Camille glanced up. "Did he tell you about the experiments?"

Zac left the window and came over to the couch to sit down. "What kind of experiments?"

"To develop all this amazing technology, Von

Meter and his cronies used human subjects,'' Camille said grimly. ''At first they used indigents that they took off the streets and sometimes military personnel who had no families, no one to ask questions when they disappeared for long periods of time. They tortured them, both mentally and physically, until they broke them so thoroughly that their minds were easily manipulated. Then they reprogrammed them with engineered realities that allowed the subjects to accept a truth that reached far beyond our three-dimensional perception of the universe. Interdimensional phasing, psychokinesis…even time travel. All of these things became possible once those three-dimensional barriers were broken down. In the face of such astonishing technology, what did a few lives matter?''

''The good of the many outweighs the needs of the few,'' Zac muttered.

''Yes,'' Camille said bitterly. ''I'm sure that's how Von Meter justified it. But he can't justify the children,'' she whispered. ''Nothing can justify that.''

''What children? What are you talking about?''

''You see, they eventually found out that children were more susceptible to the engineered realities and altered states of consciousness than adults. So they began to use younger subjects. Some of the children came from military personnel, some came from people who worked for the project. Others…they simply took.''

''Kidnapped, you mean.''

''Yes. And then they tortured them, too. As they grew older, they trained them in the art of war and turned them into super soldiers, men who would go to extraordinary lengths to carry out a mission.''

''An army of secret warriors,'' Zac said.

''Exactly. When they cut them loose, some of the men couldn't cope. Most of their memories were gone, and they had no families to go home to. They were simply…lost.''

Zac stared at her for a moment, as if he wasn't sure whether to trust her or not. ''Where do you fit into all this?''

''I work for my grandfather. He's always felt a responsibility toward these men, and he's made it his life's work to seek them out and try to return some normalcy to their lives. Now it's my life's work, too.''

''You're a crusader then,'' he said softly.

She shrugged. ''I've never thought of myself that way. I'm just trying to do the right thing.''

A shadow flickered in his eyes. ''Is that how we met?''

''No, not exactly. We met in Los Angeles. That's

where my grandfather and I live. That's where the headquarters of our organization is located. I was crossing a street one day, and I wasn't paying attention. Too much on my mind, I guess. Anyway, I walked in front of a car, and if the driver hadn't stopped in time, I would have been killed or badly injured. He missed me by inches. But somehow I knew that it had been more than the driver's reflexes that saved me. Then I saw you.'' Camille paused, remembering. ''You were standing away from the crowd that had formed on the street, and you were staring at me with such fierce concentration that I knew. I knew you were the one who had saved me. You stopped that car…with your mind.''

Zac frowned. ''I doubt that. I don't have that ability.''

''Yes, you do,'' Camille insisted. ''You may not be aware of it, but it's there, buried somewhere inside you. I saw it with my own two eyes.''

Zac's frowned deepened, as if he didn't much care for what he was hearing. ''Maybe you saw what you wanted to see.''

''It was more than that. By the time I made it through the crowd, you were already walking away. So I followed you. When you went into a coffee shop, I went in, too, and invited myself to join you.''

He almost smiled at that. "Did I object?"

Camille smiled, too. "No. You didn't. We talked for a long time, but it only took a few moments for me to realize that I'd been right. You were like all the others who'd been through Montauk. You had the same gaps in your memory, the same reluctance to talk about yourself. The same intensity in your eyes. And yet…there was something different about you. Something that…made me care about you from that very first day."

He turned and it seemed to Camille that his gaze softened as he studied her. She wondered what he was thinking.

"So what happened?" he finally asked.

"We started seeing each other. I didn't tell my grandfather about you at first because I foolishly thought that I could save you myself. And when I finally told him, he tried to warn me that I was playing with fire. Only I wouldn't listen. Then one day you just…disappeared."

"Disappeared?"

"I woke up one morning and you were gone. I never saw you again."

"Did you try to find me?"

"I did at first. Then I found out about Adam and I decided it was best that I let you go. I didn't want Von Meter or anyone at Montauk to find out I was pregnant. I was afraid they might try to use our child to keep you under their control. Or worse, do to Adam what they'd done to you.''

The haunted look in his eyes tore at her heart. ''You had him alone then? You raised him by yourself?''

''My grandfather helped me. And it wasn't hard. Adam was a wonderful little boy. Easygoing and loving...'' She trailed off at the quick stab of pain in Zac's eyes. The same pain that tightened like a fist around her heart. ''I didn't think that you would ever know about him. But you did. Somehow you found out...'' Her voice hardened. ''I suppose that was Von Meter's doing, as well.''

''Why would he do that? What would he hope to gain by telling me?''

''I don't know. Maybe he thought he could use Adam against you somehow. Or maybe he wanted to make sure that the bond between a father and a son wasn't as strong as his hold on you. When you saw Adam, your reaction must have frightened him. Why else would he have ordered Adam killed?''

Zac's head snapped around. ''*Killed?* You said he was struck by a car. It was an accident.''

''It was no accident.'' Camille got up and walked over to the window to stare out. She didn't want to think about any of this anymore. She didn't want to relive that terrible day now because she knew she would relive it again when she fell asleep.

"What happened? Tell me."

She closed her eyes as Zac came up behind her. She spoke slowly, haltingly, her every word a sword thrust through her heart. "There was a man…in the park that day. Adam saw him first and pointed him out to me. He was…watching us. I knew instinctively that he was dangerous. I wanted to leave, but Adam begged me to play baseball with him. Just for a little while, he said. And he asked for so little. He was such a good kid…." She drew a hand across her face. "A ball got away from him. He ran into the street after it."

"Then it was an accident," Zac murmured.

"No." Camille clenched her hands into fists. She could feel her nails digging into her palms, but she didn't care. "He *made* the ball roll into the street. He knew Adam would run after it."

Zac took her arms and turned her gently to face him. "That man in the park… What did he look like?"

"He was youngish, in his thirties maybe, but he had silver hair. And there was something strange about his eyes."

Zac's grip tightened on her arms. "Vogel."

Camille stared at him in shock. "You know him?"

"I've met him. And I promise you one thing." Something dangerous sparked in Zac's eyes. "Our paths will cross again, mine and Vogel's. You can count on it."

"I WANT TO ASK YOU ABOUT something you mentioned earlier," Zac said a little while later. He had returned to the couch, but Camille remained standing, as if too restless to sit. He could see her reflection in the window, and could tell from her forlorn expression that she was still thinking about her son. *Their* son.

An image of the boy came to Zac suddenly. The child was playing in the shady backyard of an old two-story house near the ocean. Zac couldn't hear the surf, but he could taste salt in the air. And smog.

He didn't even know how he'd gotten there. He didn't even know where he was. It was like a dream. All he knew was that something had compelled him to that house, to that yard, to that boy.

The child saw him, and, casting an anxious glance toward the house, started toward him. "Hello," he said when he neared Zac. "Are you here to see my grandfather?"

"I'm...not sure."

"Are you lost?" the little boy asked solemnly.

"I think I might be."

The boy reached for his hand. "You want to come inside and ask my mom for directions?"

Zac smiled down at him wistfully. "I don't think that'd be a good idea. She probably wouldn't like you talking to strangers. Besides…I have to go."

"Okay. I hope you find your way home, mister."

"I hope so, too," Zac whispered, watching the child dart away.

The image faded, and he heard Camille say worriedly, "Zac? Are you okay?"

He glanced up. "Yeah. I was just…remembering something."

She came back to the couch and sat down beside him. "You said you wanted to ask me something."

The vision had shaken him, and it took Zac a moment to collect his thoughts. "You said earlier you'd come here to protect your grandfather."

"That's right."

"From me."

She nodded.

"I'm not here to hurt your grandfather, Camille. Or you."

She bit her lip. "Then why are you here?"

"Von Meter said that on the eve of the Philadelphia Experiment, your grandfather tried to sabotage the generators on board the *Eldridge*. Is that true?''

''Yes. He'd tried everything else in his power to stop the experiment. He wrote letters to congressmen. Even appealed directly to the president. But no one would listen to him. Not until they saw for themselves the condition of the crew. By then it was too late.''

''Listen to me, Camille. This is important. Whatever your grandfather did to those generators made it impossible for them to be shut down properly once the ship rematerialized. When they continued to run, the wormhole was able to gather enough energy to stabilize. My mission is to make sure those generators get turned off. That's why I need your help. I have to get to your grandfather before it's too late.''

She drew back in shock. ''There's no way I'd ever let you anywhere near my grandfather.'' At his stunned look, Camille winced, but she didn't take it back. She couldn't. She had a mission, too. ''Look, you may really believe that shutting off those generators is your mission's objective, but I don't buy it. Think it about it, Zac. Why would Von Meter want to destroy the wormhole?''

''Because it could be the end of us all if the wrong person came through that wormhole.''

"That's true. But he wasn't concerned with that when he sent a hundred and something men to their deaths in order to recreate the Philadelphia Experiment. In order to open up a new tunnel."

Zac frowned. "What are you talking about?"

"When the *Eldridge* rematerialized, it left a wormhole that linked the past to the future. Had anyone known of its existence in 1943, he or she could have traveled forward in time. *But not the other way around.* That's an important distinction. In order for someone from the future—our present—to travel back in time, another wormhole had to be created, one that linked up with the first. That's why you and the others were on board that submarine that went down in the North Atlantic. You were recreating that first experiment. But instead of traveling forward in time, you went back. You opened up another wormhole. When the sub rematerialized, there was an explosion that sent the ship crashing to the ocean floor, trapping everyone inside. We believe that someone deliberately detonated a device in the engine room so that there would be no witnesses to what had happened."

"But I survived."

"You and the other members of your team. But don't you see? If Von Meter truly wanted the tunnel destroyed, why would he have gone to so much trouble and expense, not to mention the cost in human lives, to open a new passage? To link the present with the past? He's not trying to protect history. He's trying to change it for his own benefit by getting rid of the one obstacle that has stood in his way all these years.''

Zac's features hardened. ''Your grandfather.''

Camille nodded. ''I think you were given a false objective, Zac. I think your real mission is to destroy my grandfather.''

''Someone flashes me the queen of diamonds and I turn into an assassin?'' he said lightly, but there was no real amusement in his tone.

Camille nodded. ''Something like that.''

He glanced at her curiously. ''So if your hunch is right and Von Meter sent me here to take out your grandfather, I guess that's where things get interesting between us. You were sent here to stop me.''

''Yes.''

''How?''

The look in his eyes made Camille shiver. She returned his stare without flinching. ''I'm prepared to kill you if I have to.''

''WELL, I SUPPOSE THAT'S putting it bluntly enough. Any idea how you'll do it?''

"This is no laughing matter," Camille said with grim resolve. "I can't let you near my grandfather. I can't let you do anything to change history."

"But we've already changed history. We've changed history just by being here."

"Yes, but if we're careful—"

"Careful?" Zac gave her an incredulous look. "It's too late for careful, Camille. You changed history when you pulled me out of that mine. I changed history when I saved Billy from drowning. But would you have had me do it any different?"

She turned away from him. "No, of course not."

"And that brings up another intriguing question. If you came here to kill me, why didn't you make it easy on yourself and leave me in that mine?"

"It wasn't that simple. I had to find out for sure that Von Meter was the one who sent you. I had to know what you were up to. And besides, if I'd left you there, he would have sent someone else to replace you."

"Exactly. That's why we have to close the wormhole. If he really wants your grandfather dead, then he'll keep sending someone back in time until he succeeds."

Camille had thought about that, too. But closing the wormhole would trap her and Zac in 1943. Had he really thought that through?

And would it be so bad? a little voice whispered. With the wormhole destroyed, Von Meter would have no control over Zac. The two of them could—

Could what? Camille asked herself harshly. Start over? It was too late for that.

"We can't change history, Zac. It's too dangerous."

"It's too dangerous to do nothing." He ran a hand through his hair in exasperation. "You say you've come here to protect your grandfather from me. What if I'm not the only threat?"

"What do you mean?"

"I'm talking about crates full of explosives. What do you think they're going to do with all that dynamite, Camille? There's enough TNT in that mine to take out the whole city, your grandfather included."

"There won't be an explosion. We know that from history."

His gaze deepened. "But what if we're the ones who are supposed to stop it?"

The question stopped her cold. "We can't be."

"How do you know? It's like I said earlier, our very presence here has changed everything. What if the FBI or the police or whoever stopped the saboteurs the first time around become so preoccupied with investigating *us* that they ignore the real threat?''

Camille stared at him helplessly. ''What exactly are you proposing we do?''

''We find out who's responsible for stockpiling those explosives and what they plan to do with them. And if necessary, we stop them.''

''And how do we do that?''

Zac shrugged. ''In order to get close enough to plant the explosives, they'll need someone working with them behind the fence. Someone with a high-level security clearance. You can keep your eyes and ears open for any suspicious behavior behind the fence, and, in the meantime, I'll stake out the mine.''

Camille got up and started to pace. ''Actually, I'm already concerned about someone at work,'' she admitted. ''A woman named Alice Nichols. She befriended me when I first came to the reservation. I thought at first that she was just one of those gregarious types who makes friends with everyone, but for the past few days, I've had the feeling she's watching me.''

''You think she's on to you?''

''I don't see how she could be. My credentials and cover are solid. Grandfather made sure of that.'' Camille turned to Zac. ''But that's not all.

The other day, an FBI agent came to see me at work. He asked a lot of questions about you. He even wanted me to spy on you.''

Zac's gaze sharpened. ''What was this agent's name?''

''Talbott.''

He nodded grimly. ''Yeah, we've met. He came to see me in the hospital.''

''What did he want?''

''Just to make sure that I knew he'd be watching me.''

Camille started to pace again. ''I don't like this, Zac. You don't suppose…''

''What?''

''You don't suppose someone else came through the wormhole, do you? Someone who's trying to blow our covers.''

He thought about that for a moment. ''It's possible. But it's not unusual for the FBI to be suspicious of strangers. Especially in wartime. Especially in the vicinity of a top secret nuclear lab.''

''I suppose you're right.'' Camille tried to shake off her unease. ''I guess that could explain why I saw Talbott and Alice in the cafeteria together after he'd talked to me, but I got the distinct impression that they knew each other. And then Alice dropped a piece of paper on the floor and when Talbott retrieved it, he put it in his pocket rather than returning it to her.''

''You think she's passing secrets to him?''

''I don't know. But she told me once that she's seeing a young research assistant from my grandfather's lab. And she knows something big is going to happen on the fifteenth.''

''She said that?''

Camille grew pensive. ''The more I think about it, the more I'm starting to believe that Alice is the one we need to watch. And I haven't even told you everything.'' She turned. ''I saw her and Talbott again today. They'd arranged to meet in the supply closet at work.''

''Could it have been a lovers' assignation?''

''Maybe. But I followed her again this afternoon. She got off the bus in Ashton, walked several blocks over and then got into Daniel Clutter's car.''

''Clutter?'' Zac whistled. ''Sounds like Alice Nichols likes to get around. An FBI agent, a research assistant and an engineer who all have high-level security clearances behind the fence. Are we starting to see a pattern here?''

''So what do we do about it?'' Camille asked worriedly.

''Keep your eye on her,'' Zac said. ''But be careful. Don't let her know that you're on to her. If she feels cornered, she could be dangerous.''

Camille stared at him for a moment. ''I don't know about this. I don't know about any of this. We're not supposed to interfere, Zac. Any little thing we do could have devastating consequences. We can't just go around changing history like that.''

''Yes, we can.'' He got up and walked slowly toward her. ''We have the power to change the future, to alter the course of history. Think about it, Camille.''

She was thinking about it. Or trying to. But he wasn't making it easy. He was standing too near, gazing down at her in a way that made her breathless.

Camille wanted to back away from him, but she knew if she didn't stand her ground now, she would never trust herself with him again. She had to prove to herself once and for all that she was over Zac Riley. That he couldn't hurt her again.

But the moment he put his hand to her face, something stilled inside her. Her heart began to pound, and her knees grew weak just looking at him.

He lifted the locket to her neck and fastened it beneath her hair. When it was back in place, nestled in the hollow of her throat, he touched it with his fingertip. "We have the chance to make things right."

Was he talking about the world...or the two of them?

"Some things aren't meant to be," she whispered.

His gaze lifted. "Do you really believe that?"

"Yes." She closed her eyes. "I have to believe that. I couldn't make it through the day if I didn't believe that."

He bent then and kissed her, and it was all Camille could do not to respond. She didn't pull away, but she didn't kiss him back, either, and when he lifted his head, his gaze burned into hers. "Kiss me, Camille.

"I can't. If I kiss you..."

"What?"

She swallowed. "If I kiss you, I'll be lost."

"I'm lost, too," he said, and then he kissed her again.

HE DIDN'T BREAK THE KISS even when he picked her up and carried her into the bedroom. Or when he set her on her feet and began to untie her robe. He didn't stop kissing her as he pushed her nightgown down her arms and over her hips to puddle at her feet. He didn't stop kissing her as she fumbled with his belt and then his zipper. He didn't stop kissing her…because Camille wouldn't let him stop.

She clung to him desperately, kissing him so deeply and so utterly that Zac could feel whatever willpower he might once have had ebb away. He wanted her. Now. He wanted her hot and trembling in his arms. He wanted to be inside her, watching her face as she climaxed….

She pulled him down on the bed, and their arms and legs entangled as she kissed him again. Over and over.

When he finally pulled away, her gaze met his in the moonlight. "I want you," she whispered.

"I want you, too. More than you'll ever know."

HE KNELT AT THE FOOT of the bed. Camille lay on her back, gazing up at him through hooded eyes as he encircled her ankle, then slowly glided his hand up the length of her leg. Bending, he kissed the back of her knee, skimmed his lips along her inner thigh until Camille began to tremble violently. She couldn't stop. She plunged her hands into his hair and pulled him up to her.

"You're so beautiful," he murmured, sliding into her.

Camille closed her eyes as she arched her hips to meet him. *Yes, yes,* she thought in desperation. This is what she wanted. What she'd been missing for so long. Zac's body on hers, in hers, making her feel as if the two of them *were* meant to be.

They took it slowly at first, and then as they kissed again, their movements became more frenzied. Soft moans and whispers mingled in the darkness. Zac clasped his hands with hers, and she clung to him fiercely as their gazes met. And, for a few glorious moments, time stood still.

SOMETIME LATER, Camille lay spooned against Zac's warm body, her head cradled in her hand.

"Are you sleeping?" he asked softly.

"No, just thinking."

"About what?"

She sighed. "Adam."

Zac's arm tightened around her. "I thought so. I was thinking about him, too." The deep sadness in his voice caused tears to burn behind Camille's lids.

She rolled over and nestled her head against his chest. "I can only imagine what this must be like for you. Since it happened, life's been a living hell for me, but I wouldn't want the pain to go away if it meant losing my memories of him. I'm sorry you don't have those memories."

Zac cleared his throat. "I'm sorry, too. I'm sorry I wasn't there to save him."

Camille glanced up at him. "It wasn't your fault. There was a time when I convinced myself that it was, but I know now that placing blame on you was easier than facing up to my own guilt. I was there...and I couldn't save him."

Zac smoothed back her hair. "You can't blame yourself."

"But if I'd listened to my instincts...if I'd made him leave the park when I knew we should..." She closed her eyes. "He begged me to stay and I didn't have the heart to say no."

"Because you loved him. You wanted to make him happy."

"And now he's gone."

Zac was silent for a moment. "We've got a score to settle, Camille."

She lifted her head. "Von Meter?"

"And Vogel. They won't get away with what they've done. I promise you that."

"You can't take them down. They're too powerful. They'll kill you."

"We'll see." His mouth thinned cruelly, giving Camille a glimpse of the super soldier inside him. The super soldier who would do anything to succeed at his mission.

Chapter Twelve

After Camille left for work the next morning, Zac went back up to the mine to make sure the crates hadn't been moved overnight. He had no idea what the would-be saboteurs' time frame or target might be, but the proximity to Oak Ridge made the plants a fair bet. And if they'd somehow gotten wind of Project Rainbow, it was conceivable that Dr. Kessler's laboratory could be targeted. And that meant Camille could be in danger, as well.

Zac knew that he would do everything in his power to protect her, but what if that wasn't enough? He hadn't been able to protect Adam.

A knot of pain formed in Zac's heart, but he wouldn't let himself dwell on that now. There was too much to do, too much at stake, and he couldn't afford to distract himself—torment himself—with questions about what might have been.

He couldn't afford to think about Camille, either, and how their night together might affect his mission. He still had every intention of making sure those generators were turned off after the *Eldridge* rematerialized because, in spite of Camille's reservations, leaving the wormhole was too dangerous. Which meant he still had to find a way to get to Dr. Kessler. Preferably with Camille's cooperation, but if not...

Finding the crates undisturbed, Zac searched through several of the nearby tunnels, but locating nothing else suspicious, he went back to the cottage to set up surveillance. From the west-facing windows, he watched the ridge through field glasses, hoping to detect any movement that might be out of the ordinary.

He stayed at the windows throughout most of the day, then late that afternoon, when the shadows on the ridge grew longer and deeper, making the surveillance more difficult, he went outside to hike back up to the mine.

Billy was outside waiting for him. He came running with his ball and glove. "Hey, Zac, wanna play some catch?"

"I can't today. I've got some errands to run." At Billy's crestfallen look, Zac knelt. "What's the matter? Can't you get the twins to play with you?"

"They're not home. Mrs. Fowler sent Donny into town, and Davy went back up to—" He broke off, his eyes widening in apprehension as he realized his blunder.

"Davy went where?" Zac asked suspiciously.

"Nowhere," Billy mumbled, glancing away.

Zac put his hand on Billy's shoulder, forcing the boy to look at him. "Billy, did Davy go back up to the mine?"

He shook his head vigorously, but his eyes gave him away. He couldn't quite meet Zac's gaze.

How the hell had that kid slipped by him? Zac wondered. He'd been watching the trail all day. And if Davy had gotten by him, who else might have?

His grip tightened on Billy's shoulder. "Billy, this is important. Did Davy go up to the mine?"

Billy's bottom lip began to tremble at Zac's harsh tone.

"Just tell the truth, son." Zac tried to soften his tone. "You don't want Davy to get hurt, do you? Is he at the mine?"

Billy nodded miserably. "He'll be mad at me for telling."

Zac squeezed the boy's shoulder. "You did the right thing. That mine is a dangerous place. Your brother could get seriously hurt up there." Especially if enemy saboteurs caught him snooping around those crates. "I'm going up there to find him. I want you to go home and wait for us. Understood?"

Billy nodded and gulped. "Yes, sir."

"Good. Now take off." The sooner he got to the mine, Zac thought grimly, the sooner he could put the fear of God into Davy Clutter.

Collecting a flashlight and his weapon from the house, Zac hurried up the trail, keeping a careful watch for any other signs of life. Pausing just inside the mine's entrance, he listened for a moment before turning on his light. He heard nothing but the usual sounds at first—the constant drip of water, the creaking of ancient timbers. And then from somewhere deep in the mine came the clang of something metal hitting the floor.

Zac was pretty sure he knew where that sound had come from. Following the railroad tracks back into the mine, he made the same trek he'd made earlier that morning.

He approached the opening with caution. Light emanated from inside, and he could hear someone moving about. Flattening himself against the wall, Zac glanced around the corner, expecting to see Davy inside. But the person feverishly working at the crates was female.

She had her back to Zac, but he thought he recognized the blond hair and slender figure.

He drew his weapon and stepped inside. "Put your hands up and turn around slowly."

The sound of his voice startled her so badly, she jumped and dropped the crowbar. It landed with another loud clang against the floor.

Her trembling hands lifted high in the air, Betty Wilson slowly turned. When she saw who he was, her first reaction was one of relief. "Zac! Oh, thank goodness it's you—" Then she saw his weapon and her gaze widened. "Wh-why do you have a gun?"

"What are you doing here?" he countered. "What do you know about those crates?" He maneuvered himself into the room so that he could watch both the entrance and Betty.

"Oh, are they yours?" she asked innocently.

Zac gave her a cold glare. "I think you know who they belong to. I think you helped him move them in here three days ago."

Her blue eyes rounded even wider. "I didn't! I swear I didn't know anything about them until he brought me here last night."

"He?"

She blushed and glanced away. "Look, can I..." Tentatively, she lowered her arms.

"Keep your hands where I can see them," Zac warned.

She clasped her fingers together in front of her. "It's not what you think. I only met him a few days ago when he came to the hospital to see you. We went out a few times. Nothing serious. I just wanted…to have a little fun, and there aren't many eligible men around in case you hadn't noticed."

She paused and drew a long breath. "Anyway, after we'd gone out a few times, he told me he had contacts. He could get things for me, nylons and sugar and things like that. And all I had to do was keep an eye on you, let him know if you did or said anything suspicious. It sounded exciting at first, all cloak-and-dagger." Nervously, she moistened her lips. "But I would never have told him anything about you, Zac. Nothing important."

Zac's gaze darkened. He didn't believe her, of course. Not for a moment. "You never told me his name."

She opened her mouth to answer, but a loud crash brought on a scream instead. The lantern had somehow fallen from the peg, and, as the glass smashed against the floor, the kerosene exploded.

Zac rushed to stomp out the flames before they could spread to the crates. Out of the corner of his eye, he saw a shadow move in the doorway, but, before he could turn to defend himself, something struck the back of his head and he staggered forward in agony.

CAMILLE SAT AT HER DESK and wondered what Zac was doing at that very moment. She didn't want to think about him, but she couldn't help herself. She didn't want to think about what last night might mean for her future, because, deep down, she knew it meant nothing at all. Zac had left her once before. There was no reason to believe he wouldn't do so again as long as he was under Von Meter's control. How could she put herself through that again?

And yet…how could she not? How could she turn her back on him when a part of her still believed that she could save him?

You're a fool, a little voice warned her.

"Camille Somersby?"

She glanced up to find a young man she'd never seen before standing in front of her desk. He wore a dark suit and a badge that identified him as being from the Security and Intelligence Division. "Yes?"

"Would you come with me please?"

Camille's heart quickened. "What's this about?"

"Just come with me, please."

Reluctantly, Camille got up and followed him

into the hall, but, even away from the curious stares of the other clerks, he still wouldn't answer any of her questions. He led her down a series of corridors and stairwells until they were so deeply beneath the building Camille wondered if she would ever find her way out.

Finally the agent stopped in front of a door, knocked once, waited a moment, then motioned for her to enter. The moment she walked inside, Camille expected a bright light to hit her eyes, one so blinding that she wouldn't be able to see the faces of her interrogators. Instead, the guard nodded to one of his colleagues, then led her through two more sets of doors and finally into a laboratory containing long rows of electronic equipment with complicated-looking gauges and meters.

At the far end of the room, her grandfather sat at one of the low tables, head bowed to his work. He wore a white lab coat over his rumpled suit, and he looked up anxiously when he saw Camille approach.

"I apologize for the subterfuge." He waved the guard away and stood. "I thought it best that Special Agent Talbott not get wind of this meeting."

"Why? What's this about?" Camille asked nervously.

He rubbed the bridge of his nose as if trying to

massage away tension. "I wanted to speak with you about those letters you typed for me yesterday."

"What about them? I haven't told anyone if that's what you're concerned about," Camille assured him.

He shook his head. "I didn't think that you would. No, I wanted to talk to you about…the content. Did you understand the meaning of those letters?"

Camille hesitated, not sure how much she should tell him. She understood everything, but he wouldn't expect her to. "I gather you're trying to get members of a congressional oversight committee to stop some kind of experiment involving a U.S. warship."

He let out a weary sigh. "I shall fail, of course, just like all the other times that I've tried to appeal to their conscience—" He broke off and shook his head sadly. "There's no stopping it, I'm afraid. But…that's not the reason I wanted to see you."

"Then what is it?" Camille asked in confusion. She didn't have a clue why he'd summoned her there.

"I had you brought here because there are very few people on the reservation that I can trust. You're one of them." Before Camille could respond, he put up a hand. "I know that must sound strange. I barely know you. But I consider myself a good judge of character, and, from the moment I first saw you, I knew I could rely on you. Don't ask me to explain it. I simply knew that you were the one who could help me.''

''Help you do what?''

He reached inside his pocket and withdrew an envelope which he handed to Camille. It was addressed to a Miss Elsa Chambers at a prominent university in California.

She glanced up. ''I don't understand. What is this?''

''I've been doing a great deal of thinking about the advice you gave me. That I should get in touch with Elsa after the war, I mean. And I've come to the conclusion that you were right. I should very much like to rekindle our…acquaintance, but, unfortunately, that may not be possible.''

''Why not?'' Camille asked in alarm. Something in her grandfather's tone, in his demeanor, worried her a great deal. He had the look of a man with a monumental weight on his shoulders.

''The experiment that I referred to in those letters is scheduled to take place in a matter of days. If, as I predict, my pleas once again fall on deaf ears, there is only one thing left for me to do.''

Destroy the generators, Camille thought.

Should she tell him the truth? Should she try to convince him that his one final act of desperation and defiance had the potential to change the world in ways he couldn't even begin to imagine?

"What are you going to do?"

His eyes glinted with steely determination. "If I can't prevent the experiment from taking place, then I shall be a part of it."

Camille stared at him for a moment. "What are you talking about?"

"I plan to be on board that ship to witness first-hand what chaos is wreaked when man decides to play God."

Camille gasped as the implication of his words sank in. "But you can't do that. You can't be on that ship."

Her reaction clearly startled him. "It's something I have to do, for my own conscience. But, you see, I don't know what the outcome of the experiment will be. No one does. That's why I want you to make sure Elsa gets that letter. I want her to understand why I left things the way I did—"

Camille flattened her hands on the table and leaned toward him. "Don't you understand? Your presence on that ship could change everything. It could have consequences you can't even begin to imagine. The world needs you alive. *I* need you. I won't let you do it, Grandfather. Do you hear me?''

He looked at her in astonishment. *"Grandfather?"*

ZAC WAS PRETTY SURE he'd been out for only a few minutes, but during that time, he'd been dragged across the dirt floor, his arms pulled behind him and fastened with handcuffs around one of the old wooden support beams. Betty was behind him, her arms pulled back and secured to the brace, as well.

Another lantern had been brought in, and Zac glanced around, trying to pinpoint his attacker.

"He's gone," Betty whispered.

"I have a feeling he'll be back," Zac muttered. Using the handcuffs, he tugged at the beam, and a shower of dirt and gravel rained down on them from above. Very clever, he thought. If they struggled too strenuously to free themselves, the whole mine could come down on them.

"Are you okay?" he asked Betty.

"Yes. He didn't hurt me. What about you? He hit you pretty hard."

"It was just a glancing blow."

"Glancing blow?" she said in disbelief. "You were out cold. For a moment there, I was afraid…''

"Good thing I have a hard head, I guess." Zac

frantically glanced around for something to use as a weapon or to pry loose the handcuffs. If he could just reach that crowbar with his foot—

A shadow appeared in the doorway just then, and as Zac's gaze lifted, his blood went cold.

The silver hair. The odd-colored eyes.

"Vogel." He all but spat the name. And then something Camille had told him the night before came rushing back to him. *"It wasn't an accident. He made him run into the street after the ball."*

A fury like nothing Zac had ever experienced came over him, and he knew beyond a shadow of a doubt that had he been free at that moment, he would have ripped the man's heart out with his bare hands.

As it was, Zac jerked helplessly at the handcuffs, accomplishing nothing more than to trigger another tiny avalanche of dirt.

Vogel laughed. "Quite a predicament you find yourself in, isn't it? Struggle too hard…and the mine could cave in on you. Ingenious, if I do say so myself."

"What the hell are you doing here?" Zac growled. "Did Von Meter send you?"

"Von Meter doesn't call the shots for me. He hasn't in a long time."

"Then why are you here?"

"Right now? I'm putting the finishing touches on some rather clever explosives I've devised for my new friends." Vogel walked across the room and took something out of one of the crates, placing it gently inside the leather bag he'd brought in with him. Then he straightened. "The Germans have quite an impressive network in this area. They've even got people behind the fence, and they're quite eager to deal. I've already made some very useful contacts, but then, why wouldn't I? I'm one of them, see. My grandmother was a German spy. Or rather, *is*. She's been operating in Oak Ridge for nearly a year now, right under the very noses of the FBI."

Zac continued to work at the handcuffs. He could feel Betty doing the same. "Who is she?"

"A clever young woman named Alice Nichols. She has no idea who I am, of course. I'm saving that little tidbit for just the right occasion." He grinned down at Zac. "Actually, you've met her. You probably don't remember, but she paid you a visit in the hospital. If it wasn't for Nurse Betty there, you would never have awakened from your coma."

Betty said in outrage, "So she *was* trying to smother him with a pillow that day. I *knew* it!"

Vogel laughed. "Can you blame her? He's been

quite a nuisance. She actually wanted to finish you off, too,'' he said to Betty. ''But I convinced her you could be useful to us. A little flattery, a few baubles, and you were more than willing to spy on Zac for me, weren't you? Of course, that's over now. I'm afraid you've outlived your usefulness.''

''What are you going to do to us?'' Betty demanded, but the tremor in her voice gave away her terror.

''That'll be up to Zac.''

Zac cut him a glance. ''Meaning?''

Vogel came over and knelt beside them. He held up a key, then tossed it to the floor a few feet away. ''You've always been Von Meter's fair-haired boy even though I had ten times the skills and talent. Time after time you led missions that should have been mine. But all that's about to change. You see, Zac, you were never really a match for me. Not in the future and not here in the past. Look how easily I got the best of you.''

''It's not over yet,'' Zac said.

Vogel grinned. ''That's the old fighting spirit.'' With his toe, he slid the key a few inches farther away. ''Let's see how much of a super soldier you really are. You once had some rather mundane telekinetic skills. How about it, Zac? Can you move the key?''

Zac stared at the key for a moment, wondering what the hell he was supposed to do. According to Camille, he'd once had the power to stop a speeding car with his mind. Now he didn't even have a clue how to move something as tiny as a key.

As if reading his mind, Vogel laughed again. "That's what I thought." He stood and walked back over to the crates.

"You say Alice Nichols is your grandmother." Zac tried to focus his attention on the key. "What about your grandfather?"

"I've never known who he was," Vogel said matter-of-factly. "Someone my grandmother used to get information on the Allies, no doubt."

"What arrangements have you made with the Germans?" Zac still had his eye on the key. Was it his imagination, or had it moved a millimeter? Behind him, Betty gasped softly, and he wondered if she'd seen it, too.

"They're willing to pay millions to find out the secrets behind the fence. They'll pay even more for the secrets of Project Phoenix. And all I have to do is deliver Dr. Kessler to them. Preferably alive, but if that isn't possible, his notes will suffice."

A cold chill shot through Zac. Vogel planned to kidnap or murder Nicholas Kessler. And the person standing in his way was Camille. She would die protecting her grandfather. Zac knew that without a doubt. He also knew that he would do everything in his power to make sure that didn't happen. He hadn't been able to save Adam, but he damn sure meant to save Camille. Or die trying.

Closing the leather bag, Vogel picked it up and walked to the entrance. Turning he stared down at Zac. "In a matter of minutes, when I'm safely down the ridge, I'll detonate enough explosives to seal the entrance of this mine, as well as your fate. This time, you won't be leaving here alive."

"If you blow up the mine, you won't be able to go back through the wormhole. You'll be trapped here," Zac said.

He shrugged. "The Germans will treat me as a god once I deliver victory to them. They'll lavish me with riches and power beyond my wildest dreams. I think, under the circumstances, I'll be able to adjust." Then, with a mocking salute, he turned and disappeared into the tunnel.

"What was he talking about?" Betty asked nervously. "The future, the past? What did he mean by that? And how did you make that key move?"

"You saw it move?" Zac asked anxiously.

"Of course, I did. How on earth—" She broke off as the key moved again, another millimeter.

"How did you do that?" she asked fearfully. "Who are you people? *What* are you?"

Zac tried to tune her out as he concentrated on the key, but it didn't help. He could move the key slightly, but not enough. The fierce meditation only left him light-headed.

"How long before the explosion, do you think?" Betty asked worriedly.

"Not long." With renewed determination, Zac focused on the key. There had to be a trick to it, some way to harness his energy—

"Zac?" a voice whispered from the main tunnel.

"Davy?"

The boy glanced over his shoulder as he crept through the opening. "I think he's gone."

Fear shot through Zac as he realized the danger the kid was in. "Davy, you have to get out of here. He's put a bomb in here somewhere."

But instead of running away, the boy scrambled across the floor and picked up the key. Quickly, he unfastened Zac's handcuffs, then Zac in turn freed Betty.

The young woman looked shell-shocked as she rose shakily to her feet. "What do we do now—"

It started with a low rumble that began to build until the sound grew deafening and the floors and walls trembled. Dirt and rock spewed down on them, and dust thickened the air until Zac could see no more than a foot or two in front of him. His throat and eyes stinging from the assault, he reached out blindly and found Betty, found Davy, then pulled them both toward the opening. "Come on! We have to get out of here!"

"There's nowhere to go," Betty screamed. "He blew up the entrance. We're trapped in here—"

Davy tugged on Zac's arm. "I know another way out."

He darted into the main tunnel, and Zac followed, pulling Betty with him. Behind them, he could hear the log braces snapping in two as the tunnels began to collapse.

Chapter Thirteen

"Answer me! Why did you call me 'grandfather'?" Dr. Kessler demanded. His blue eyes burned into hers.

"Because I—" Camille's head snapped around at the sound of a distant explosion. The equipment on the table rattled for a moment as her heart started to pound in alarm. "What was that?"

"It sounded a long way off," her grandfather said. "Whatever it was, I don't believe we're in any danger."

Camille wished she could be as certain. But she remembered all those crates stacked in the mine and Zac's assertion that there could be a threat, other than from him, against her grandfather's life.

She glanced up in panic. "I think we should get you out of here."

"I beg your pardon?"

"Off the reservation. Out of Oak Ridge. It's not safe for you to be here right now."

He frowned as he regarded her across the table. "You never answered me. Why did you call me that? I'm obviously not old enough to be your grandfather. Is it some sort of code? Who are you? Something tells me that you're no ordinary file clerk."

"No, I'm not," Camille admitted. "I've been sent here to protect you."

His eyebrows rose in surprise. "Sent by whom?"

She paused. "I was sent here by…you."

He gave her an incredulous look. "That doesn't make any sense at all. I sent for you, yes, but not to protect me. I told you, I want you to deliver a letter for me—"

"And I told you, you can't be on that ship when it disappears. It's too dangerous."

"When it disappears," he repeated. His gaze narrowed in suspicion. "How do you know about that? I never mentioned anything specific in those letters that you typed. How do you know—"

"That the ship will vanish? Because you've made other objects disappear here in the lab, haven't you? You've devised generators that create electromagnetic fields around objects, rendering them invisible. Except…they're not just invisible.

They're transported to another time, another dimension...and when they return, they're altered somehow. That's why you're so worried about the experiment scheduled to take place on that ship. You've already seen what can happen.''

He sat down heavily in a chair, his face drained of color. ''How can you know this? How can you know any of this?''

''The experiment will go off as scheduled,'' Camille said. ''And when the ship rematerializes, it will punch a hole in the space-time continuum, forming a tunnel that will link your time—1943— to the future. And sixty years from now, the experiment will be recreated using a submarine. Another tunnel will be formed that links the future to...now. To 1943.''

He stared at her as if she'd taken leave of her senses. But there was something in his eyes, a glint of fear, that made her think a part of him already knew she spoke the truth. ''What are you saying? That someone from the future could travel back in time?''

''Not just in time. To *this* time. To 1943.''

''That's not possible.''

''Yes, it is,'' Camille said softly. ''I'm living proof that it is.''

He put a hand to his mouth and observed her for

a long, tense moment. "You're trying to tell me that you're from the future?"

"I'm trying to tell you more than that." She gave him a tentative smile. "I'm trying to tell you that I'm your granddaughter. And I've come here to protect you."

He drew a sharp breath. "My...granddaughter? That's ludicrous. As I said before, I'm obviously not much older than you."

"But sixty years in the future, you will be. It's true," Camille said softly when he didn't respond. "You said yourself, you knew from the moment you laid eyes on me that you could trust me. Don't you see? There's a reason for that. We have a bond. We're family. You're my grandfather. Or you will be."

He lifted a hand and ran it through his hair. "How do I know this isn't some elaborate hoax? Some enemy ruse—"

"It's not a hoax. I'm your granddaughter." Camille reached across the table to touch his hand, but he jerked away from her. She drew a breath. "Okay, I see I've got my work cut out for me. So here goes. After the war, you'll not only become reacquainted with Elsa Chambers, the two of you will marry and have a daughter whom you'll name

Elizabeth, after your mother. My great-grand-mother. I'm Elizabeth's daughter.''

He was looking at her not so much with suspicion now, but awe. "You do remind me so much of Elsa," he murmured.

"The two of you will have a long and happy life together," Camille said.

Something sparked in his eyes. "She…is still alive? In the future, I mean?"

Camille shook her head sadly. "She died a few years ago."

"And your mother? Elizabeth?"

"She's gone, too. And that's why you can't get on that ship. You're all I have left—" Camille put out her hand again, and this time he didn't pull away. "If you get on that ship, there may not even be a *me*. If you die, I die, too. My mother and my son… There won't even be memories because we'll never have existed."

He closed his eyes. "What do you want me to do?" he whispered.

"Don't get on that ship. The experiment must take place as it did before."

His eyes flew open. "But all those men… They'll die…"

"And more will die in the future. Lives will be ruined because of the technology you created, but we can't change that. We can't tamper with the future. We can't play God. You told me that once.''

''A very noble sentiment.'' A door closed somewhere behind them and Camille turned. Her breath caught in her throat as her gaze lit on the man walking slowly toward them.

''How did you get in here?'' her grandfather demanded. ''Where's Agent Wilkins?''

''The man you had stationed at the door? He's…incapacitated at the moment.''

A chill shot up Camille's backbone at the implication of his words, and as his gaze met hers, she knew exactly where she'd seen him before. She was looking into the eyes of her son's killer.

''You *bastard*.'' Camille lunged for him, but he quickly drew his weapon and she knew that he wouldn't hesitate to use it. Not for a moment. She froze, but fury raged in her heart. She wanted to kill him more than she'd ever wanted anything in her life. But revenge would have to come later. For now, she had to protect her grandfather. ''What do you want? Why are you here?''

''I want Dr. Kessler to come with me.''

Camille glared at him. ''Over my dead body.''

Vogel shrugged. ''That could easily be arranged. Or would you prefer that I put a bullet in him and simply take what I need? It's of no consequence to me, but I should think it would be to you.''

''Who are you?'' Camille's grandfather came around the table to stand beside her. He put a protective hand on her arm. ''What do you want?''

''I told you. I want you to come with me. But first, I need you to gather up all your notes and files, everything you have on Project Rainbow. Then you and I are going to take a long trip.''

''Where?''

''Berlin, ultimately.''

''You'll never get away with it,'' Camille said. ''You won't make it out of this building, much less out of the country.''

''Oh, I think we will,'' Vogel said. ''Most of the guards have been conveniently distracted by the explosion. Those who get in our way will be dealt with. And, of course, there's the tunnel that you and your colleagues use to slip in and out of the city,'' he said to Dr. Kessler. ''Very clever of you.''

Camille tensed, but her grandfather's hand tightened on her arm, as if warning her against attempting anything foolish.

''In a matter of minutes, we will be outside the fence,'' Vogel told them. ''I have someone waiting with a car to take us to a nearby airstrip. From there we will fly to the coast and rendezvous with a U-boat in the Atlantic.''

Camille quickly stepped in front of her grandfather. He tried to shove her aside, but she stood her ground. ''He's not going anywhere with you. You'll have to kill me first.''

''An easy fix,'' Vogel said and took aim.

''Freeze!''

To Vogel's credit, he didn't even flinch as the door to the lab banged open. It was as if he'd been expecting the intrusion all along.

''Drop your weapon!'' Special Agent Talbott shouted. He came slowly into the room, his gun leveled at Vogel's back. ''Turn around slowly,'' he ordered.

Vogel began to turn. He lowered his weapon to his side, but he didn't drop it.

''Put it down! Now!''

Vogel continued to turn.

''Drop your weapon or I'll shoot,'' Talbott warned.

''You're not going to shoot me, Agent Talbott.''

Talbott's finger tightened on the trigger. ''Don't be too sure about that.''

''But I am sure. If you were going to shoot me, you would have already done so. Like this.'' In the blink of an eye, the gun flew from Talbott's hand.

He didn't even have time to utter a shocked gasp before Vogel lifted his weapon and fired.

Talbott staggered back against the wall, clutching his chest. When he brought his hand away, his fingers were covered in blood. His gaze lifted to Vogel, and then, as if in slow motion, he slid down the wall to the floor.

THE SOUND OF GUNFIRE chilled Zac to the bone. Camille!

He had been following the maze of corridors and stairways that he'd memorized from the blueprints Von Meter had given him, but he hadn't been certain he was heading in the right direction until he heard the shot.

And if he'd heard the gunfire, so had the guards. Within a matter of moments they would converge on Kessler's laboratory, and Zac would have a hard time convincing them that he was on their side. Especially after having used the diversion of the explosion to slip behind the fence.

If the guards came, he'd have to deal with them, he thought grimly. Right now, his first concern was Camille. And her grandfather.

Hurrying down another stairway, he saw an open doorway at the end of a long corridor. Loud voices were coming from inside. When he recognized Camille's, he let out a breath of relief. Thank God, she was still alive. This time, he wasn't too late. Not…yet…

Pressing himself against the wall, he inched toward the doorway.

"He's still breathing," he heard Camille say. "But if we don't get him to a doctor, he'll die."

"You're all going to die," Vogel said calmly. "And we may as well start with you."

"Vogel!"

He whirled at the sound of Zac's voice, his face contorting in fury. And then his expression turned to shock as his own weapon flew from his hand.

"It's just you and me, Vogel." Slowly, Zac walked into the room. He refused to meet Camille's gaze for fear of losing his concentration, but he could see her out of the corner of his eye. She knelt on one side of Talbott, her grandfather on the other as they took turns applying pressure to the dying man's wound.

Zac observed all this in the split second before he lunged for Vogel. His hands wrapped around the man's neck and then, locked in a death grip, they went crashing against a table filled with expensive equipment.

IT WAS AN UGLY STRUGGLE. A bitter fight to the finish. Camille's heart was in her throat as she watched them, knowing that one man would not walk away.

Zac seemed to have the upper hand at first. Perhaps he'd caught Vogel sufficiently off guard, but the man quickly recovered, and he broke Zac's grasp on his neck. Then he grabbed Zac's throat and the two of them fell back into another table.

Camille spotted Talbott's gun on the floor and scrambled for it. She leveled it at Vogel, but, in the space of a heartbeat, he and Zac had switched positions. It was impossible to get off a clear shot.

The fight seemed to go on forever with neither man gaining the clear advantage. Then, as they thrashed on the floor, Vogel's hand closed around a metal pipe and he swung it against Zac's temple. Zac's arm flew up to shield his head, but the pipe still connected. Stunned, he fell back against the floor, and, before he could recover, Vogel was on top of him. Somehow he'd gotten his hands on a long, jagged piece of glass and his intention was clear. He meant to slash Zac's throat. He drew it back, and in the split second before he brought it down, Camille fired.

For a moment, she wasn't sure she'd hit him. She

fired again, but the bullet seemed to pass right through him.

And then before her very eyes, Vogel began to…disappear.

"HE'S DEAD."

Camille slowly turned to find her grandfather still kneeling beside Talbott. Then she rushed to Zac.

He sat up and shook his head, as if to clear his vision. "What just happened?"

"I'm…not sure," Camille said. "I shot him. Or at least, I think I did. The he just…disappeared. Vanished." There wasn't so much as a drop of Vogel's blood left on the floor.

"What the he—" Zac's words were cut off by a gasp from the doorway. They both spun to find Betty Wilson and Davy gaping at what they'd just witnessed.

Betty's terrified gaze went from Zac to Camille, then back to Zac. "Who are you people? How did you… How did you do that?"

Davy appeared speechless for a moment, then his eyes rounded in excitement. "You really are from the future! Donny's never gonna believe this!"

With an effort, Zac got to his feet, then both he and Camille walked over to the dead man. Dr. Kessler stared up at them. "He disappeared at the exact moment Agent Talbott stopped breathing."

Camille put a trembling hand to her mouth. "Then he must have been—"

"Vogel's grandfather," Zac finished. "He said his grandmother is Alice Nichols. Or she would have been. She and Talbott must have hooked up during the war, but she never told anyone about it. Talbott probably never even knew she was pregnant."

"And by killing his own grandfather, Vogel ceased to exist." Camille clutched Zac's arm. "That means—"

He shook his head. "Don't. We don't know what it means. We don't know how the future has been changed by what we've done tonight."

Dr. Kessler said grimly, "He's right. The tunnel you told me about earlier, the one that opened up after the experiment…I can see now how dangerous it is. It must be destroyed. We can't take the chance that someone else like him—" he nodded to the spot where Vogel had disappeared "—could come through it. And as for you two… You have to go back. Now. You can't stay here. Look at the damage you've already done."

Camille stared at him in shock. "But we saved your life. That's why I came here."

Her grandfather glared at her. "Then your mission has been accomplished. It's time for you to go. Both of you."

"He's right," Zac said. "The explosion sealed off the entrance to the mine, but Davy knows another way in. If we don't go now, it may be too late. The tunnels are collapsing. The whole mine could go." He turned to Kessler, quickly explaining what had to be done to the generators aboard the *Eldridge* once it rematerialized.

"I understand," Kessler said impatiently. "Now go."

Just then, Betty rushed up to Zac, threw her arms around his neck and kissed him long and hard on the lips. Zac pulled back, stunned. "What was that for?"

"Where you're going, I'll be an old lady. Or dead. I figured that was my last chance."

Camille looped her arm through Zac's. "You got that right."

Betty grinned good-naturedly, then said, "Oh, I almost forgot. I found this in the mine. I think you must have dropped it." She pulled a gold medallion from her pocket and handed it to Zac.

He stared at it for a moment, then turned to Dr. Kessler. "Actually, I think this belongs to you."

Dr. Kessler took the medallion from him and

held it up to the light. The gold chain sparkled as it swung gently to and fro. "It's lovely," Kessler said. "But it's not mine. I've never seen it before—"

Camille's heart actually stopped beating when she saw the look on Zac's face. He was focused intently on the medallion, and she knew, suddenly, that the trigger planted in his subconscious had been activated. She lifted Talbott's gun at the exact same moment Zac lifted his own weapon. It was a standoff.

Her heart pounding against her chest, Camille's finger tightened on the trigger. "I can't let you do it," she whispered.

He seemed not to hear her. His gaze was still focused on the medallion.

"Don't do it," she pleaded. "If you kill him, you kill me. I'll disappear just the way Vogel did. I'll cease to exist. Is that what you want? For us to have never been together?"

When he didn't so much as blink an eye at her plea, Camille said desperately, "What about Adam? Think about it, Zac. He could be alive now. He could be in the future, waiting for us. All we have to do is go find him. Put down the gun, Zac. Please. For Adam's sake…"

Without a word, Zac dropped his arm to his side

and the weapon fell to the floor. Only then did his gaze meet Camille's. And what she saw shining in those dark depths made her want to weep.

THE HOLE THAT LED DOWN into the mine was barely large enough for an adult to shimmy through. Zac went first, dropping the five or six feet to the floor and then lifting his arms to assist Camille as she came through.

The air was thick with dust from the collapsing tunnels, and the walls and floors still trembled from the aftershock of the explosion. They inched their way along the narrow passage, stepping over debris and at times having to stop to clear the way before they could go on.

As they neared the wormhole, Camille's heart started to pound in excitement. She took Zac's hand and squeezed. "Do you really think it's possible—"

"I don't know. I'm almost afraid to think…to hope…" He turned to stare down at her. "Let's just take it one step at a time."

She nodded. He was right. One step at a time. And the first step…was to make it back home.

"Ready?" Zac asked her.

She drew a deep breath and nodded.

And that's when they heard it. A voice calling out to them. For a moment, Camille thought—

Her gaze flew to Zac's. "Is that—"

"It's Davy. He must have followed us into the mine."

"Oh, my God." Camille glanced around frantically. "The tunnels are still collapsing. He'll be trapped in here—"

She stumbled and lost her balance as the floor shifted beneath her feet. Davy called out again, this time in panic.

Zac grabbed Camille and lifted her to her feet. "Go!"

"No! I'm not leaving without you!"

"Go find Adam!" he shouted. "Go find our son!" And with that, he pushed her through the wormhole, and the last sound Camille heard was the roar of collapsing rock and debris.

Chapter Fourteen

Camille awakened to strange faces peering down at her. She tried to sit up, but gentle hands pushed her back down. "Take it easy now. You're going to be fine."

She blinked in confusion. "Where am I?"

"You're in Memorial Hospital in Knoxville. You were brought into the emergency room after some tourists found you unconscious near an old mine shaft just outside of Oak Ridge. Do you remember what happened?"

She put a hand to her head. Everything was still so foggy. Oak Ridge? A mine shaft?

"You had some rather strange-looking papers on you," the doctor commented. "They dated back to 1943, and we assumed you were part of a documentary film crew that's staging a reenactment nearby. Does any of that ring a bell for you?"

Camille shook her head.

"What about a man named Nicholas Kessler? Do you know him?"

Camille gasped as memories started rushing back to her. Oak Ridge. The mine. Zac!

She tried to sit up once again, but the doctor wouldn't have it. "Take it easy," he advised. "You've obviously been through something pretty traumatic."

"Zac?" she asked frantically. "What about Zac? Did he make it through?" He had to have made it through. He had to!

The doctor and nurse exchanged glances. "As far as we know, you were alone. About Dr. Kessler... He says he's your grandfather...."

Camille fell back against the pillow. "Where is he? I have to see him."

"He's on his way from California. He should be here in a few hours."

"Did he—" Camille swallowed. "Did he say anything about Adam?"

"No. Who's Adam?"

She squeezed her eyes closed as a deep sorrow welled inside her.

WHEN SHE OPENED HER EYES, he was sitting on the edge of her bed. She thought it was a dream at first, but the image seemed so real, that day in the park might never have happened.

And then everything shifted. As she gazed at her son, Camille was assailed by memories…memories of the past year…memories of her and Adam at a baseball game…on a picnic…walking him home from school…

Memories…as if he had never been gone…

Camille put out a tentative hand to touch him. "Adam?" she whispered in wonder. "Is that really you?"

"Who do you think I am? The tooth fairy?" He giggled then, as if his joke were the funniest thing in the world, and Camille had never heard anything in her life sound so wonderful.

She laughed, too, and pulled him into her arms, hugging him so tightly, he had to squirm to get free. "Mom, stop it!"

But she wouldn't stop. She wouldn't let him go. She clung to him so fiercely that he finally relented and hugged her back. And it was the most precious feeling in the world to Camille.

It was as if that day in the park had never happened. Because it hadn't…

"COME ON, MOM! YOU PROMISED!" Adam prodded her.

"I know, but…" Camille glanced around. The park still terrified her. That long-ago day was nothing more than a dream now, but she couldn't shake the awful sense of foreboding she always experienced when they came there to play.

Adam took her hand and squeezed. "Mom, who's that man over there? And why's he looking at us?"

"What man?" Camille's gaze lifted, and her heart began to pound when she saw him. The shadows obscured his face, but Camille knew that he was watching them.

"Zac?" she whispered.

He watched them for another long moment, then turned and walked off.

"COME IN, MR. RILEY. Dr. Von Meter is expecting you," the maid told him.

"He is?"

"Of course. May I take your coat?"

"No, I think I'll keep it, if you don't mind." Never knew when you'd need to make a speedy exit, Zac decided. He glanced up. There was no snow on the skylight today. Sunshine streamed in through the glass, easing Zac's feeling of claustrophobia.

The maid ushered him down a long, dim corridor

to a set of ornate wooden doors which she swung open with a flourish.

"Dr. Von Meter, Mr. Riley is here to see you."

The old man stood at the window staring out at the garden. He didn't speak until he heard the doors close behind the maid, and then he said over his shoulder, "I've been waiting for you."

"Have you?" Zac walked slowly toward him.

The old man turned. When he saw the look on Zac's face, something that might have been fear flashed in his eyes. "Stop," he said. "Don't come any closer."

Zac kept walking. "We've got a score to settle, old man."

"I don't know what you mean—"

"You know exactly what I mean. If you, or anyone associated with Project Phoenix, goes near Camille or my son again, I'll kill you. Do you understand?"

With an effort, Von Meter seemed to muster his dignity. "How dare you speak to me in such a manner? I'm the one who created you. I control you...."

Zac reached out and closed a hand around Von Meter's throat. "News flash, old man. You're not God. It's time you stopped pretending that you are."

CAMILLE SAW HIM FIRST THIS TIME. He stood in the shadows, watching them. And just like before, her heart began to pound as he moved out of the trees into the sunlight. Their gazes met, and she felt everything inside her go still.

Adam came running over and tugged on her arm. "Who is that man, Mom? I've seen him before."

"Have you? Where?"

He shook his head in confusion. "I don't know."

Zac started walking toward them then, and Camille's heart beat even faster. She didn't think she'd be able to utter a word, but when Zac stood before them, she whispered his name.

"Von Meter is dead," he said.

Camille caught her breath. "Did you—"

He shook his head and glanced down at Adam. "Hello, there."

"Hello."

Zac knelt, his heart in his eyes as he gazed at his son. "I've been watching you play. That's some arm you've got."

Adam beamed. "You wanna play catch with me?"

"Sure. Baseball's my favorite sport. That is…" He glanced up at Camille. "If your mother doesn't mind."

"I don't mind," Camille said softly. She sat

down on a nearby bench and as she watched them through a veil of tears, time seemed to stand still. Her gaze met Zac's and he smiled. She heard her son laugh, and she captured the moment in her heart. Then the world began to turn again. Time moved on.

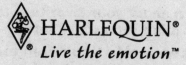

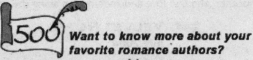

USA TODAY **bestselling author**

ERICA SPINDLER

Jane Killian has everything to live for. She's the toast of the Dallas art community, she and her husband, Ian, are completely in love—and overjoyed that Jane is pregnant.

Then her happiness shatters as her husband becomes the prime suspect in a murder investigation. Only Jane knows better. She knows that this is the work of the same man who stole her sense of security seventeen years ago, and now he's found her again... and he won't rest until he can *See Jane Die*...

SEE JANE DIE

"Creepy and compelling, *In Silence* is a real page-turner."
—*New Orleans Times-Picayune*

Available in June 2004 wherever books are sold.

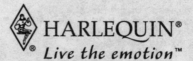

If you enjoyed what you just read,
then we've got an offer you can't resist!

Take 2 bestselling love stories FREE!

Plus get a FREE surprise gift!

Clip this page and mail it to Harlequin Reader Service

IN U.S.A.
3010 Walden Ave.
P.O. Box 1867
Buffalo, N.Y. 14240-1867

IN CANADA
P.O. Box 609
Fort Erie, Ontario
L2A 5X3

YES! Please send me 2 free Harlequin Intrigue® novels and my free surprise gift. After receiving them, if I don't wish to receive anymore, I can return the shipping statement marked cancel. If I don't cancel, I will receive 6 brand-new novels each month, before they're available in stores! In the U.S.A., bill me at the bargain price of $3.99 plus 25¢ shipping and handling per book and applicable sales tax, if any*. In Canada, bill me at the bargain price of $4.74 plus 25¢ shipping and handling per book and applicable taxes**. That's the complete price and a savings of at least 10% off the cover prices—what a great deal! I understand that accepting the 2 free books and gift places me under no obligation ever to buy any books. I can always return a shipment and cancel at any time. Even if I never buy another book from Harlequin, the 2 free books and gift are mine to keep forever.

182 HDN DU9K
382 HDN DU9L

Name	(PLEASE PRINT)	
Address	Apt.#	
City	State/Prov.	Zip/Postal Code

* Terms and prices subject to change without notice. Sales tax applicable in N.Y.
** Canadian residents will be charged applicable provincial taxes and GST.
  All orders subject to approval. Offer limited to one per household and not valid to current Harlequin Intrigue® subscribers.
  ® are registered trademarks of Harlequin Enterprises Limited.

INT03

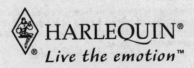

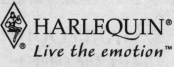

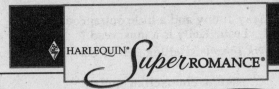

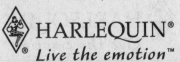